BY THE SA.   ~~AUTHOR~~

Frog

Frog and the Sandspiders of Aridian

To

OSCAR

FROG AND THE TREE OF SPELLS

JOFFRE WHITE

Matador
9 Priory Business Park,
Wistow Road, Kibworth Beauchamp,
Leicestershire. LE8 0RX
Tel: 0116 279 2299
Email: books@troubador.co.uk
Web: www.troubador.co.uk/matador
Twitter: @matadorbooks

ISBN 978 1784625 405

British Library Cataloguing in Publication Data.
A catalogue record for this book is available from the British Library.

Printed and bound by CPI Group (UK) Ltd, Croydon, CR0 4YY
Typeset in 12pt Aldine401 BT by Troubador Publishing Ltd, Leicester, UK

Matador is an imprint of Troubador Publishing Ltd

Dedicated to the memory of
Bob, Nickie, Wendy and Norman.

Acknowledgements

My grateful thanks to –

Pat Drinkwater – Use of golden tree sculpture
on front cover.
www.patrickdrinkwater.co.uk

John Whitcombe – Photograph of golden tree.

Julia Suzuki – Author of Land of Dragor.
www.juliasuzuki.com

PRELUDE

FROG – THE ADVENTURE BEGINS

On a summer evening in the school holidays, twelve-year-old Chris Casey finds himself at a loss. His friends are away for their annual holidays and he has only his cat, Tabby, and his mother for company. To console himself he searches the sky for his favourite constellations, knowing that his love of astronomy may be all that will keep his boredom at bay in the coming weeks. He could not be more wrong. Investigating a mysterious object that appears to have fallen from the sky, and into the orchard of his garden, Chris encounters a knight transported from another Dimension, and is soon taken there himself. His arrival in the medieval world of Castellion leads Chris into an exciting, terrifying adventure, in which he will gain a new identity – Frog – and play a central role in the future of both this Dimension and his own. Here, he meets the first of the Guardians, the wizard Gizmo, and is gifted with the powers of the Chosen. He learns of his quest to stop the evil Lord Maelstrom from conquering the Four Dimensions. With the help of his newfound stable companions, Fixer and Ginger, along with the fearless Lady Dawnstar, the formidable Sir Dragonslayer, and a mysterious ranger known only as Logan, he must travel into an underground labyrinth and seek out the ancient and mystical Earth Sage, in a race against time, before Lord Maelstrom's hideous army, and dark magic enslaves them all.

FROG AND THE SANDSPIDERS OF ARIDIAN

At thirteen, and another year older, Chris Casey returns as the legendary 'Frog'. The Guardians call upon him again to fight the abominable Lord Maelstrom and his sister, the wicked Belzeera. In the second Dimension of Aridian, a scorched, desert world where most of the population lives underground, he meets new allies including the young Nadiah and her energy-wielding girls of the Sisterhood, along with a mysterious character known only as The One. A new Guardian, in the guise of the beautiful Cassaria, is on hand to aid him with her magic. Frog's journey takes him into the depths of Aridian, from the spider hatcheries at Pelmore to the wonders of the subterranean ecosystems of Arachnae. Amongst his encounters are giant spiders, the ugly Saurs, the aggressive Dreden, the enchanting Firefox and the revered Sandspider Arac-Khan. Find out what happens when evil turns true friends into enemies, and join him as desperate foes and monstrous creatures pursue him at heart-stopping and breakneck speeds through the underground waterways and caverns of Aridian. Only one thing is predictable: Frog and his adversary, Lord Maelstrom must face each other again to discover what destiny has in store for them and the future of the Dimensions. Even when his life hangs in the balance, will those around him keep their faith in one boy's ability to survive against the odds?

1.

The Third Dimension

A steamy rainforest; the air reverberates with a wild chorus of nature echoing down from the tropical canopy and up from the lush damp undergrowth. Trees and plants glisten, dew-dropped and moist with the humid environment. Shafts of light streak through tall, long-limbed trees to reflect from broad leaves and dapple in patches of shaded groves. Rising up in the distance is the snow-capped peak of a slumbering volcano. Somewhere from the undergrowth, there comes the excited laughter of children playing. This is a strange paradise where bright colours flourish everywhere. Red. Orange. Yellow. Green. Blue. Indigo. Violet. Every colour of the rainbow – vivid, brilliant, and alive.

The sun is a purple-blue disc, and at the beginning of every day, it appears high in the sky, in the same place. When dawn arrives, it is immediate, as if a light is switched on. The sky turns white, and orange clouds periodically materialise to deliver showers of glistening raindrops, before they are ushered away by warm tropical breezes.

When night comes, it is instant. A solitary silver moon hangs effortlessly amongst constellations of bright, flickering, celestial stars.

This is Tropal, the third Dimension, and something is coming to this paradise.

Something unwanted.

Something evil.

2.

INCY WINCY SPIDER

Life has pretty much settled down to normality, and it was nearly six months since Chris Casey returned home from his quest in the second Dimension of Aridian.

It still felt weird to him, having shared the last adventure with his father, and even weirder now that he knew Chris' secret. His mother, his father had advised him, still did not need to know about it, saying that it would only worry her, particularly if there were the possibility of Chris going back into the Dimensions. They both agreed that with the added threat of the evil Lord Maelstrom's existence, secrecy was the best policy – for the time being.

After a cloudy and rainy July, summer finally arrived – with a vengeance. Over the last few days, the heat had become unbearable. A national health warning about spending too much time in direct sunlight had been issued by the government. Hosepipe bans were in force and the long-term forecast was for much more of the same dry, hot weather. Shops had sold out of electrical fans, and ice cream manufacturers could not make their confectionery fast enough to keep up with demand.

On this hot Saturday afternoon in August, Chris lay on his bed in a t-shirt and boxer shorts. He wafted a hand-held mini fan in front of him; its plastic blades whirred precariously close to his nose to deliver the soft relief of moving air. The bedroom curtains were drawn against the sunlight, and the window yawned open wide in an effort to gasp any suggestion of a breeze into the room.

His thoughts were preoccupied with deciding what to do next month on the occasion of his fourteenth birthday. If the weather didn't cool down it looked like he and his friends would be spending the day at the beach – it would be far too hot for paintballing!

He absently stared at the ceiling, trying to make pictures out of the white-painted, swirled and stippled pattern; it was then that the remains of a dream from the previous night crept into his conscious thoughts.

The foggy image of a familiar face drifted into his head. One amber eye looked out clear and alert, opposite a crimson red eye patch, which covered an empty socket where another healthy eye used to reside. The trace of a white scar zigzagged across a furrowed brow to travel behind the patch and down onto the cheek. It was Logan, a companion and dear friend from the first Dimension of Castellion. In the dream, Logan was leaning over Chris' bed and looking down at him; he was saying something that Chris couldn't quite make out. Logan's voice and the words from his lips were lost as if they were whispers on the wind.

Chris screwed his eyes up and tried to force the dream back into his head, but just as he thought that he heard Logan's voice, the images scattered from his mind like a frightened flock of birds.

Disappointed, he opened his eyes and continued to stare up at the ceiling, when a tiny movement caught his attention. It was a spider. Not the dark, plump, hairy version usually seen running for cover across carpeted floors. This was a spindly long-legged one, which wobbled its way unsteadily to a point above Chris' head. He turned off the fan and watched in fascination as the spider tilted its body head-down. Slowly, it lowered itself on a thin strand of spider silk, until it was suspended at eye level to him, centimetres from his face.

Every detail of the spider's head was clear, as though Chris was looking at it through a magnifying glass.

He felt a tingling sensation on his arm, and he looked down to see that the black spider tattoo on his skin had once again become the solid bracelet that Arac-Khan had presented to him on Aridian.

A young girl's soft voice entered his head.

Hello, young Frog.

Chris glanced around his bedroom.

There is no one else here except for you and I.

'Where are you?' asked Chris.

Here, in front of you, and please do not use your voice. You should know by now that it scratches and scrapes inside a spider's head. Use your telepathy.

Chris sank his head further back into his pillow and stared at the small creature, which hung motionless in front of him. He sent out the thought. *It's you! You're the one speaking to me?*

That's better. I have a message for you from the Guardians.

You have a message for me from the Guardians? echoed Chris.

I do hope that you are not going to repeat everything I say.

Sorry, it's just a bit of a shock, Chris explained.

You have spoken with spiders before, on Aridian. Why not in your own Dimension?

I guess it's because I've never thought that I could.

Well, you know now. So listen. Many years have passed on Aridian and all is still well there; however, the third Dimension of Tropal is now under threat. Lord Maelstrom has used the Rune Stone of Aridian to restore some of his powers. He is nowhere near as strong as he used to be and he is still mortal, but he is searching for the Tree of Spells. He has found out that it is concealed somewhere on Tropal. *The Tree of Spells gives absolute power to the holder, and should it ever come into his possession, then we will all be truly doomed. At the moment, the magic of the Ancients keeps it hidden from all, even from the Guardians themselves. It was never intended to be given to any one person and let them have such knowledge and power.*

You want me to go to Tropal and try to stop him? Chris guessed.

We need you to find the Tree of Spells and bring it to this world for safekeeping. The Guardians have discovered a prophecy that says only the Time Child can be trusted to move and hide the Tree of Spells, without corrupting its powers. The Time Child and the boy called Frog are one and the same. Both are you my friend.

Chris' head spun. He had just got used to being called Frog, in the Dimensions, but now this 'Time Child' thing? It was getting so complicated.

Frog! Concentrate. All of your random thoughts are clouding my head!

Sorry. I guess it's this heat that's distracting me.

He brought the fan up to his face again and flipped it on.

Whoa! The spider's voice yelled in his head, as the breeze blew it sideways like a pendulum.

Sorry. Chris panicked and he fumbled for the tiny switch to turn it off, but he was too late and the spider sailed off onto the crumpled duvet.

Where are you? Chris' eyes darted frantically across the cover.

Don't move. I'll climb onto your leg.

Chris watched patiently as the small creature appeared on his knee, like a multi-limbed stilt-walker. It was just then that Tabby decided to jump onto the foot of the bed. The cat caught sight of the spider and moved towards it with curiosity, a playful gleam in its eyes.

I think that you will be safer in my hand. Chris gently scooped up the spider and lightly brushed the cat to the floor with the back of his hand. 'Sorry, Tabby.' The cat gave a meow of displeasure before it rolled onto its side and started to groom itself.

Chris turned and sat up, his legs resting over the side of the bed. The spider nestled in his palm and Chris brought it up level with his face.

Yes, you are needed once more to aid the Dimensions. The spider continued. *Lord Maelstrom has already brought evil to the people of Tropal, and only you can save the Tree of Spells. As always, the Slipstream will hold back time whilst you are away, and none shall miss you on your return.*

If I survive to return, added Chris.

You have self-doubts?

I'm a realist, mused Chris. *One day my luck could run out.*

You make your own luck – you take control of your own destiny. The spider asserted. *Have you learnt nothing on your travels?*

How come you know so much? Chris asked.

8

My kind has existed for millions of years; we collect and share knowledge whenever we are able. Besides, I am connected to the Dimensions. I am a messenger, and my message for you is that you are needed once again. Can you rise to this challenge? Can you answer the call?

Chris took a deep breath and cleared his head. *Of course I can. I made a promise that whenever I am needed, whenever I am called, I will come, and I keep my promises. Tell me what I must do.*

Open the body of the armlet.

Chris placed the spider onto the back of his left hand and studied the bracelet. It was in the shape of a large spider; its metal legs were wrapped around his wrist and the body was a black oval stone about the size of a fifty-pence coin. He could just make out a delicate hinge on one side. He slid his thumbnail underneath the stone and eased it upwards. Inside the small compartment was something that looked like a dried broad bean. Cautiously, he took it out and held it up between his thumb and forefinger.

What is it?

The gateway to the next Dimension – to Tropal.

Don't tell me that I'm supposed to swallow it?

No! You need to plant it and water it well; then when it has grown, you must pick its leaves and use one of them to open the Slipstream – by running it along the blade of your sword. Do not forget to take the rest of the leaves with you.

So, how long is it going to take to grow? Chris examined the wrinkled, brown seed.

9

In the time that it takes you to plant it, water it and prepare for your journey. Do not forget – things are not always as they seem.

Chris smiled. *How could I ever forget that?* He looked at his watch. *I guess that now is as good a time as any. Both of my parents are out, so I won't have to worry about being seen planting the seed, and getting my things. Are you coming with me?*

I am, but in another form. The spider crawled across Chris' hand and onto the bracelet. It settled into the empty compartment, and drew its legs in and around itself so that it nestled in a small ball. *Now close the lid.*

Are you sure?

Do not ask questions, just close the lid.

Chris did as he was told and clicked the stone cover back into place. As soon as he had done so, the bracelet melted into his arm and once again became a black tattoo.

'Weird,' he murmured as he gently rubbed it with his finger. 'Okay. No sense in hanging around.' He picked his jeans up from the floor. 'Looks like it's time for another adventure,' he said to Tabby. With a bemused expression on its feline face, the cat watched as Chris wrestled himself into the faded denims, before retrieving a pair of black and white Dunlop trainers from beneath his bed. He gently stroked the purring cat behind the ears before he left his room, and made his way down to the kitchen. There, he filled a plastic measuring jug with water, and carefully carried it outside. The heat of the summer sun glared down from a cloudless, blue sky, and his skin caught its intensity in an instant.

'Phew! Feels like another hot one,' he complained.

After collecting a small trowel from the shed, he made his way beneath the sheltering leaves of the old apple trees. He decided to plant the bean in the same spot where he had unearthed the suit of armour and released Sir Peacealot many, many months ago. Crouched on his knees, he dug a shallow hole with the trowel, and then he gently placed the bean at the bottom of it before he filled the earth back and into the shape of a small mound.

'Well, here goes,' he said quietly, as he poured the water over the soil. Rays of bright sunlight flashed like crystal rainbows as they reflected off the stream of liquid. Satisfied, he made his way to the shed, and once inside, he pulled off the dusty timeworn blanket, which covered an old chest of drawers. As dust motes danced a reckless ballet in the disturbed air, he knelt down and eased open the bottom drawer to retrieve a hidden cloth bundle. Slowly, he unwrapped it and brought out his dark green, medieval clothes, a short sword in its scabbard, a dragon-skin waistcoat, a coiled whip, and a small wooden box.

With the end of a finger, he traced the strange runes that decorated its surface, and he turned it over in his hands. There was no lid, no hinges, and no sign that you could open it in any way. He brought the box close to his lips and whispered, 'Frog.'

The top melted open to reveal a long silver chain. He held his breath as he felt along the chain until his fingers closed around an unseen talisman. His hand turned transparent. The magic worked its way up past his wrist, and began to turn his entire body invisible. He let go, and allowed himself to return to normal.

'Just checking,' he mused as he looped the chain around his neck.

Ten minutes later, he had changed into his Frog clothes: the dragon-skin waistcoat, the green, hooded cloak, and the tunic and leggings, which, he felt at times, made him look like a hobbit! His sword hung on his belt in its scabbard along with a small pouch. The leather whip was coiled, bandoleer-style, across his chest, and his normal clothes were now bundled up and placed inside the closed drawer. He took nothing personal with him, not even his watch, as he had already learnt that it was wise not to introduce objects from his world into another Dimension.

'Okay,' he breathed. 'Let's go and see if I'm any good at growing seeds.'

As he left the confines of the shed, the heat hit him yet again. He looked around, checking that there was no one nearby to see his activities. Then, satisfied that the coast was clear, he quickly made his way back to where he had planted the seed.

From between his teeth, he let out a low whistle; where he had planted the seed only minutes before, there now stood a small sapling, about a metre tall. A dozen, silver-green leaves sprouted from tiny stalks along the dark brown stem, which glistened as if coated with morning dew.

He reached out and gently touched the seedling, and it seemed to quiver in anticipation of what was to come. He felt that it was a shame to pluck the leaves from the newly grown plant, and his hand hesitated for a moment; it was then that one of the leaves stretched out and wrapped its soft blade around his fingers. Slowly, it detached itself from the stem. Chris turned his hand over, and the leaf settled into his palm. He studied it for a moment, to take in the detail of the dark, silver veins that ran along its length, before he placed it into his pouch. Seconds later it was joined by ten more. While he stood there with the twelfth leaf gently clasped in his hand, a blue-white light reached out from his sword and attracted his attention. He carefully drew it from its scabbard. As if in response, the leaf gave off an aura of brilliant white light, and it trembled again, ever so slightly.

Things never cease to amaze me, Chris thought. *There are people who don't believe in magic – they have no idea what they're missing!*

He brought the sword up and ran the radiant leaf along its length. Immediately, ancient rune scripts illuminated along the blade, and ran deep within the metal; it was then that the Slipstream opened up and a spiralling, swirling galaxy of stars wrapped around him.

'Here we go again,' he said, as the velvet black cloak of sleep invaded his consciousness.

As always, no one saw the green-cloaked figure of a boy disappear into thin air, as if a magic eraser had rubbed him out.

3.

TROPAL

Frog opened his eyes with a start. He gasped as if it were his first breath. The transformation from a normal teenage boy into the mature, rational, steely-resolved personality of Frog was complete once again.

He lay on his back in soft, green vegetation. Above him, through a covering of leaf-laden branches, he could see a pure white sky, as if bleached of all other colour.

As usual, he felt slightly light-headed and disorientated by the side effects of the Slipstream. He slowly rolled onto his side and brought himself into a kneeling position so that he could just see above the foliage that surrounded him, and as the dizziness subsided, his head cleared and he took in his surroundings.

He was in a tropical rainforest! The sound of birds exchanging their energetic chatter filled the air. The colours of the plants and flowers were so vivid that they almost hurt his eyes. He had never imagined that shades and spectrums could be so intense and have such depth.

The humidity soaked through his clothes as though someone had thrown a bucket of warm water over him. He was sweating as if he were in a sauna.

I've got to get out of these clothes, he thought, and he discarded his thick cloak. The material of his tunic was already saturated, and he wrestled to pull his arms out and wrench the stubborn garment over his head. Feeling no cooler, he sat there half naked, his skin glistening with perspiration.

There was an abrupt silence. It was as if somebody had switched off all the sound. For a moment, he thought that he had been struck deaf. Then, cutting through the air like a jagged knife, there came screams. High-pitched, frightened screams. The screams of nightmares. The screams of terrified children.

A new sound cut through the screams. The deep throaty trumpet of a hunting horn rent through the air, and the chaotic noise of the jungle exploded around him. The urgent shrieking of birds preceded the frantic beating of their wings as all manner of feathered shapes took flight and rose up amongst the trees.

The screaming came closer, and with it, the thrashing of foliage was accompanied by deep guttural, booming grunts. The turmoil of noise filled the air.

Frog drew his sword as he saw several shapes emerge from the undergrowth around him. They were young, all about the same age as him. It seemed to his eyes that they were wearing camouflage, a sort of body paint, which made them blend in with the plants and shrubbery.

He saw one figure turn momentarily, with a look of sheer panic and fear in their wide-open eyes. Frog was about to call out, when a long, green tendril shot out and wrapped itself around the stranger to bind them captive in a tight noose. Such was the strength of the snake-like vine that the youngster, still screaming, was lifted up high into the air. Then, as Frog stood open-mouthed, the tall grotesque figure of a half man, half tree strode out through the forest.

The creature, (for Frog could think of no other description for it), stood at least three metres tall. Its arms and legs were human-shaped, and it even had the semblance of a human face, which was covered in brown and green bark-like skin – cracked and deformed. However, the most disturbing feature was its two oversized, bulbous black hexagonal-patterned eyes. They were the type of eyes that were usually seen on a fly.

From its back writhed four long, vine-like tentacles, one of which dragged a large net, and it was into this that its other vines were forcing the now silent and shocked child. The creature raised its head and opened the ragged hole of a mouth. It trumpeted a deep, loud, wailing sound. 'Gooooraaah!'

Several other children emerged, pursued by more of the tree-like creatures. Some of the youngsters managed to duck and dive the flailing tendrils, and escape into the trees, whilst others were not so fortunate and were lassoed, and cruelly shoved into the nets.

Seemingly, from nowhere, a body rocketed out of the vegetation and collided with Frog, knocking him over. As he regained his senses, a girl crouched before him; her emerald green eyes were wide with surprise, her face an expression of sheer terror. She let out one word.

'Hide!'

A thought quickly came into Frog's head. 'Stay still,' he said quietly. He hugged the figure protectively.

'Keep quiet. It's going to be okay,' he whispered reassuringly.

He grabbed his cloak and pulled the garment over them, to cover them both in the dark green material. In the darkness of the cocoon, he reached inside of his tunic, and as his fingers closed around the warm, metal talisman on its chain, the transparent shield of invisibility engulfed them both.

The sound and tremor of a heavy foot crunched into the ground, centimetres from Frog's face. He heard a deep, guttural grunt come from above them, like a warthog clearing its throat, and then the creature moved on. They lay there for what seemed a long time, until the sounds of screams and blaring horns receded into the distance.

Frog slowly and cautiously peeled back the hood of his cloak and raised his head. He strained his ears and listened for any sound of warning. Satisfied, he let go of the talisman and pulled the rest of the clothing aside as they both regained their visible forms. His eyes widened with surprise at the sight of the girl, whose entire appearance now matched the colour of his cloak.

'What? Who are you?' he asked.

The girl pulled herself onto her knees, and with her pure green eyes, she studied Frog for a moment.

'I am Mystra, daughter of Sol,' she replied. She brought the palms of her hands together and up to her forehead, in a gesture of greeting.

'Well, it's nice to meet you, Mystra. I know that you must be scared, and I don't know what's happening, but I would be grateful if you can help me. I need to find the Guardian of this Dimension.'

She gasped. 'You! You are the one!'

To Frog's disbelief, the girl threw her arms forwards onto the ground, and she knelt prostrate, face down.

'What are you doing?' he asked.

'You saved me, and I am eternally thankful. It will be an honour to die for you. You are he, are you not? You are the Legend. The Chosen one called Frog. Is that not so?' came her muffled reply.

'Get up,' said Frog, as he gently lifted the girl's arms. 'You don't have to bow to me, no matter who you think I may be. I am not anyone's master. Do you understand?'

Mystra leaned back on her haunches. She smiled and nodded at Frog. As she continued to stare, her skin, hair and clothes changed from the green of his cloak to take on the hues and colours of the plants around her.

'How are you doing that?' asked Frog. 'You're like a, a – chameleon!'

'We are the colour keepers,' replied Mystra. 'We are the people of Tropal.'

'What were those creatures?'

'Drak!' came her reply.

Frog noticed that Mystra shivered as she spoke the name.

'Why are they chasing you?'

'To destroy the colours. To kill the forest. To desolate Tropal. If they catch us, they imprison us in the dark caves of the mountain.'

'But why?' asked Frog, even though he already had an idea who was to blame.

'Because the evil one searches for the Tree of Spells,' Mystra replied.

Frog took a moment to study Mystra. Now, close up, she looked about the same age as him. She had a sharp-featured face and her hair was slicked down and tied back into a long ponytail. Her clothing was a sort of sleeveless t-shirt and a short, ragged kilt. Even the colours in the material seemed to shift and change hue. Several leather-style bracelets adorned her arms and wrists. Around her waist she wore a thin leather belt, to which was attached a long cylindrical pouch and a wooden tube.

'What do you know about the Tree of Spells?' asked Frog.

Before Mystra could answer, a small, colourful bird alighted on a branch above them. It reminded Frog of a hummingbird. Its bright plumage was of every spectrum of the rainbow. It gave a low trilling whistle, before it flew off like a dart, amongst the trees. Mystra jumped up and tugged at Frog's arm.

'Come. We must go,' she said with a nervous urgency.

'Where?'

'I will take you to the Guardian. He will explain all that there is to know.'

And I have a feeling that it's not going to be good news, thought Frog as he sheathed his sword and picked up his clothes. 'Lead the way.'

They warily made their way through the

trees, which glistened with fine moisture, as did everything else in the rainforest. Frog noticed that as any leaves brushed Mystra's arms and legs, her skin changed to the patterns and hues, rippling in and out of different colours. He was so mesmerised by the effect that he lost concentration and when Mystra suddenly stopped, Frog stumbled into the back of her.

'Sorry,' he apologised.

'We need to be very careful and very quiet now,' said Mystra, in hushed tones. 'They always watch this place and they will try to stop us from reaching the Canopy.'

'What's in the Canopy?' asked Frog.

'It's where we live. You must stay close to me, and when I say to run, you run – fast. Understand?'

'Ha! Don't you worry; I certainly know how to run,' said Frog.

They crept forwards through a thicket of high, wide-leafed ferns, and as Mystra parted two of the leaves Frog could see a wide stretch of clear ground in front of them. At its centre the trunk of an enormous tree rose up. It reminded Frog of the giant Canadian redwood trees from his own Dimension. The trunk looked about three metres in width, and at the centre of its base, an open doorway was cut, like the arched entrance to a cave.

'That's where we need to go,' indicated Mystra. 'Once we get inside, there is a stairway. It will be quite dark, so make sure that you keep close to me.'

The colours on her skin started to flow and swirl, like a blend of oil and water. Browns and greens, yellows and deep reds rippled around each other.

'Run!' she shouted.

They were off, tearing across the clearing like a couple of greyhounds. Dapples of sunlight undulated across the forest floor, spotlighting their progress. About ten metres from the doorway, Frog felt the ground vibrate.

'Don't look around,' shouted Mystra.

Recklessly, Frog cast a glance over his shoulder to see the giant figure of a Drak striding towards them. Two of its tentacles writhed through the air, ready to reach out and ensnare them.

'Don't worry,' she encouraged. 'We're nearly there.'

Frog was five metres from the tree when he instinctively ducked and a green tentacle swished above his head like a scythe.

'Ha!' he shouted in response. 'Missed me!'

Before he took his next step, he regretted his words as he felt the tight grip of something entwine around his ankle. With a sharp jerk backwards, he found himself suspended head down, a couple of metres above the ground.

As blood rushed to his head, he stared at the Drak, and its encrusted face creased with what passed for a vicious smile. Multi-faceted eyes studied him and reflected hundreds of miniature images of his upside-down face back at him.

'Hold on!' he heard Mystra shout.

Hold on? Thought Frog. *That's the last thing that I want to do! I need to getaway!*

Frog tried to release his sword from its scabbard, which hung at an awkward angle against his head.

'Come on!' he shouted at it in frustration as he struggled to unsheathe the stubborn blade. With one last desperate tug, the sword came free. Without hesitating, Frog brought the glinting steel around in an arc, and sliced it effortlessly through the restraining tendril.

'Oh! That's gross!' he complained as a jet of sticky, green liquid splashed out across him.

With the vine severed, gravity had its natural effect, and Frog dropped to the floor with a thump that knocked the breath out of him. He lay there on his back, gasping for air, the safety of the doorway within arm's reach. Above him hovered the dark, knurled underside of an enormous foot, as the Drak prepared to bring it down and crush the life out of him.

Frog closed his eyes; he didn't even have enough breath left in him to scream.

4.

The Canopy

Seconds passed. Then, from overhead, he heard the angry sounds of grunts and snarls. Tentatively, he squinted an eye open to see the Drak suspended high above him. Two large branches extended from the tree in the shape of giant arms and misshapen hands that now held the creature in a vice-like grip.

Two smaller and gentler human hands reached out, and pulled Frog into the relative safety of the doorway.

'I did tell you not to look around,' said Mystra.

'I know. I know,' apologised Frog, as he regained his breath.

He looked up at the struggling Drak.

'Is this tree alive? I mean, is it helping us?' asked Frog, with amazement.

'The tree is one with us, with my people,' said Mystra. 'It is part of the Canopy and will protect us in whatever way that it can.'

As if to confirm her statement, there came a

deafening grinding and cracking sound from above them. The tree twisted and wrenched the Drak apart into two pieces like a Christmas cracker. The great limbs of the tree cast the remains of the Drak aside as if it were pieces of matchwood, and its death howl echoed through the forest like a lost, mournful ghost.

'Incredible!' exclaimed Frog.

Mystra helped Frog to his feet and led him into the centre of the tree. Rays of misty light filtered in from above to reveal a wooden spiral staircase. The small bird returned and fluttered in through the doorway, to perch on Mystra's shoulder. It cocked its tiny head to one side and studied Frog with one of its shimmering eyes. Mystra whispered something to it so quietly that Frog was not sure if she even spoke. Whatever passed between them was kept secret and the tiny creature took flight up the stairway, and its shape melted into one of the shafts of sunlight.

'Follow me,' she told Frog.

She nimbly climbed the smooth wooden steps, and Frog, (who was still a little out of breath), managed to keep up with her. He was grateful when the stairs ended and they stepped out onto a platform, which was built in a circle around the great tree. They were now about twenty metres above the forest floor. Suspended in front of them was a large conical-shaped basket, thickly woven out of dried, mustard-coloured vines and large enough to accommodate three or four people.

'Don't tell me,' groaned Frog. 'It's a lift cage, and we're going up in it.'

'Yes. It's how we get to the Canopy. Come on,' she gestured.

She stepped inside the basket and sat cross-legged on the rough floor. Immediately, her appearance changed to match the cream and brown colours of the structure.

For a moment, Frog marvelled at her natural ability to blend in with her surroundings, before his attention was jerked back to the challenge in front of him. He tentatively stepped forwards across a small gap, which was wide enough for him to see the sheer fall beneath them. He grabbed at the basket with one hand as he stumbled onto the floor next to her. Recollections of the nerve-wracking lift journey that he had experienced in the underground Dimension of Aridian came flooding back to him, and he inhaled anxiously. The basket swayed gently as if to taunt him.

'Are you afraid of heights?' asked a concerned Mystra.

'No,' replied Frog, with a nervous smile. 'Just of the fall!'

'Don't worry, we're quite safe,' said Mystra.

The word 'safe' did nothing to reassure him.

A thin length of braided, multi-coloured twine hung from the roof of the basket, and she reached up and gave it a tug.

There was a jolt, and Frog's stomach felt as though it contained the fluttering wings of startled butterflies. Slowly, they ascended; the basket creaked and squeaked in dry complaint. His only saving grace was that apart from the basket's entrance, which faced the trunk of the tree, he could not see out.

'How far have we got to go?' he asked, hoping above hope that the answer would be 'not far'.

'The Canopy is high above us, and reaches for the sky,' said Mystra. 'So just relax and enjoy the ride.'

Wrong answer. Thought Frog.

As it turned out, the journey developed into a smooth ride. There were no sudden bumps or erratic swaying, just the passing of the tree's trunk, which filled his vision. In fact, at times it seemed as if the great trunk of the tree was moving steadily downwards, rather than the basket ascending.

His mind drifted as he sat waiting to reach their destination. He thought of his father. Frog hadn't had time to leave a note or a message to tell him where he had gone. There again, he wondered if it would have made any difference. He wouldn't be missed as time stood still while he was away from home, and any message would remain unread. Then other questions crept into his mind. Should he have waited, and told his father what had happened? Was his father supposed to have come with him?

His attention was brought back to the present by a gentle vibration in the basket, and his thoughts

28

skittered away like frightened mice. The basket rose up through a circular hole in a large platform, and they came to a steady halt. Mystra was quick to her feet, and helped Frog to stand. The little bird flitted into view and hovered in the doorway, its minute wings moved so quickly that they were a blur. In a blink, it perched on Mystra's shoulder and it uttered a soft melodic trill.

She stood back and held out her hand. 'After you, Frog. A welcome awaits.'

Frog could see a number of figures in a group on the platform. He realised that he was holding his tunic and cloak in a bundle, and all of a sudden, he was very self-conscious about his semi-nakedness.

'Just a sec,' he pleaded as he wrestled to put on his clothes. The humidity and the dampness of his garments made it feel as though he was getting dressed under water. He tugged and grappled with the material, until fully clothed.

He looked like a sack of potatoes, he was drenched in sweat, and his hair was plastered to his head. *Not exactly the entrance that I was hoping to make*, he thought as he stepped forwards.

The great knurled trunk continued to disappear into the branches above, and the platform seemed to extend well out into the foliage of the tree. Several structures, which appeared to be constructed of reed or cane, were nestled amongst the tree's huge limbs. Leading off in different directions, above and below, were a number of rope walkways that interweaved with the myriad of branches and connected to even more structures, which seemed to merge endlessly with other trees. It was like a village, suspended high above the forest floor, and Frog briefly wondered how this miracle of engineering had been constructed.

A semi-circle of people waited to greet him, their faces broad with welcoming smiles. Their attire of colourful sarongs and long cloaks was embroidered with feathers, and along with their bold jewellery, the style was similar to that of the ancient Aztecs. Their skin, hair and the material of their clothing seemed to shimmer and undulate with the greens and browns of the forest. Little patches of dappled sunlight flickered amongst the hues and shades. The effect was mesmerising, and Frog did not notice as Mystra moved quietly over to stand with them.

A lean faced man stepped forwards and spoke.

'We are honoured to welcome to Tropal, the Legend, the one who is known as Frog.'

As one, the ensemble knelt, and they brought their hands to their foreheads in the same gesture of greeting that Mystra had used.

Frog stood there, very self-conscious and aware of his dishevelled appearance. The last thing he felt that he looked like was a 'Legend'. Besides, he always felt humbled and embarrassed when he was treated like this.

'Please. You mustn't bow to me. I'm just here to help. In fact, I'm not really sure what's expected of me.' He looked around, feeling awkward. 'Please. Please get up.'

'The reputation of your modesty does not fail you,' said a voice that was soft and melodic.

From out of the dappled shadows a figure emerged that had the stature and features of a man in his mid-twenties. His kind, smiling face and gentle countenance, along with his shaven head and saffron-coloured robes, gave him all the appearance of a Buddhist monk. He carried a long, polished wooden staff, the crown of which was embellished with an ornate carved hand. Grasped within the palm of the hand was a pale yellow globe.

As he walked amongst the kneeling group, they began to stand, and the effect was astounding. The colours of their bodies and garments changed. The greens and browns melted into deep violets and mauves. The transformation rippled through each figure like gentle ocean waves.

The man gave the same hands-in-prayer gesture, and then reached out and took one of Frog's hands in his.

'Welcome, young Frog. It is with both honour and trepidation that I greet you. I am Koy, Guardian of Tropal.'

Frog stood, mesmerised. He looked into the Guardian's purple eyes and it was as if every care, every worry, every fear in his mind melted away.

'I'm pleased to meet you,' he finally managed.

'Come,' said the Guardian. 'I will arrange for you to wash and have a change of clothes. You appear to have had a somewhat troublesome journey to us.' He beckoned Mystra over. 'Mystra, ensure that Frog is taken care of, and then bring him to the Cradle in time for the Afterglow.' He smiled at Frog. 'Until later,' and he moved away to talk with the patiently waiting group.

'Right, let's get you cleaned up,' said Mystra, as she took Frog by the arm and led him across the wide expanse of decking.

'I must look a right mess,' grumbled Frog as he tugged at the limp material of his cloak.

'I don't think that anyone noticed,' said Mystra, kindly. 'Besides, they were just a small welcoming party. We will meet the Council when we go to the Cradle.'

'And that's supposed to make me feel less embarrassed?' complained Frog.

'You could have been coated in Drak dung, and no one would have minded,' she smiled. 'You are the Legend that is Frog, and that is all that matters.'

'Tell me,' said Frog. 'What exactly have you heard about me?'

'We know only what the Guardian has deigned to share with us, but with every telling amongst my people, your exploits have become more well known.'

'Give me an example,' asked Frog, his ego overtaking his curiosity.

'You have flown with the Dragons of Castellion, and can speak their language,' she said, eagerly. 'And you defeated the ice army of the Hidden People, by releasing the Blackwater.' She paused. 'Oh yes! You lost the top of your little finger to the vile wolf, Fangmaster, but no one in your world can see that it's gone. Is that true?'

Frog held up his hand for her to see the shortened digit.

She stared at it for a moment before continuing excitedly. 'Personally, my favourite tale is when you met Arak-Khan and visited the spider hatcheries on Aridian.'

'The Guardian of Tropal told you all these stories?'

'Yes. Sometimes after gatherings, the Guardian allows some of us to sit with him for a while, and he educates us on the history of the Dimensions. He has been telling us of your quests for many years now.' Mystra's expression changed to a sombre one. 'We never thought that the evil one would reach Tropal. Foolishly, we always thought that we would be safe. Now he threatens to destroy us all.'

Frog stopped mid-step and put his hands on Mystra's shoulders. He looked into her eyes. Dull hues of grey and murky browns coloured her face and reflected her downcast mood.

'I promise you that I will do everything in my power to stop Lord Maelstrom from harming you, your people or your Dimension.'

In an instant, all colour bleached out of her. It was as if she had become a white spectre. A ghost. Frog stared in disbelief. He watched his own hands and the edges of his sleeves lose their colour, as if infected by whatever was happening to her. He quickly pulled himself away.

'What's wrong?' he asked, alarmed and shocked.

'You cannot speak his name when you touch any of us. Not out loud. It will cause us great harm.' She staggered back and sank to her knees.

'I… I didn't know,' stammered Frog. 'What can I do to help you? To stop this from happening to you?'

'Get some leaves from a branch. Quickly,' she pleaded. 'I must consume colour.'

She became a white silhouette, and her body started to flicker like a strobe light.

He looked around in a panic. The branches and foliage were far above his reach. Then he remembered what he had in his pouch.

He pulled out one of the silver-grey leaves. 'Here, take this!' He thrust it into Mystra's now translucent hand, and he gasped as the leaf melted into her palm.

As Mystra wrapped her arms around her knees and curled up into a little ball, he stood there, feeling totally helpless. Her body had now turned completely transparent. All of her recognisable features had disappeared.

'Help!' he shouted in desperation. 'Somebody please help!'

The sound of running feet approached from behind him, he took no notice – his gaze was transfixed on Mystra. A soft, golden glow had started to melt through her body. Gradually, it spread to every part of her, and made her whole again. She uncurled herself, and steadily got to her feet. Frog couldn't see her face at first, until she turned and looked directly at him. He stared, open-mouthed, as a burning sun – the sign of the Chosen – radiated from her forehead. Frog felt his own forehead tingle, and in response, it glowed golden and reflected the burning image.

The Guardian moved between them, and gently placed his hands on their shoulders. 'Even I did not foresee this,' he said. 'There is hope for us yet.'

5.

BLACK MOUNTAIN

The conical shape of Black Mountain rose up out of Tropal's dense forest landscape, its cratered peak permanently shrouded in murky grey clouds.

Nothing would grow on its black slopes, not even moss or the most perennial weeds. Its gullies of hardened lava and its boulder-strewn terrain were completely barren. No one would venture there. This was a source of destruction and violent rebirth.

It was no surprise then, that in its depths an uneasy darkness stirred and plotted. That darkness was Lord Maelstrom. When the Slipstream had spewed him out many years ago, wounded and mortal as a result of his previous encounter with Frog, he had taken refuge in the bowels of the mountain. He had escaped with the Rune Stone of Aridian, and the ancient parchments, which had helped him to recover some of his powers. It was a slow process, and he had to use the most basic elemental magic to help him.

He had crawled deep into the ancient core of the mountain, to where the molten, blood-red lava flowed and bubbled, and was content to remain below ground – for now. It was here that he had started to revive his sorcery. He called upon the buried bones of long-forgotten souls. He beckoned ancient, dark-dwelling creatures to awaken and come to his side, and eagerly, they came. Blind, slithering, foul, macabre entities. They surrendered to him, and he gave them no reward. He used them as tools for his dark magic. He ground them up and drained their essence. He wallowed in their deaths. Their sorrow and agony fed his strength and gave him a new malevolent beginning.

Now, although his powers were only a fraction of his previous abilities, Lord Maelstrom's domain inside the caves and tunnels of the mountain had grown. He commanded the first creatures of his making – the Drak.

His ambition to dominate the Four Dimensions, and enslave all its peoples, burned deep in his mind. This was now fuelled by his thirst for apocalyptic revenge against those who had destroyed his sister, the evil witch, Belzeera. That revenge was focussed against the Guardians and also towards a particular meddling boy. He knew that eventually the boy, the one called Frog, would have to return. It was their fate to meet again.

Lord Maelstrom swore by all the dark arts that

this time it would be different. He was searching for the Tree of Spells – the ultimate instrument of power. In his ruthless quest, he intended to destroy the forest. When everything else had shrivelled and died, he would find the Tree of Spells. It would be his for the taking, and no one would stop him.

He had busied himself, scrutinising the Rune Stone of Aridian and the ancient parchments, and it was from these that he had discovered a long-hidden secret: the Tree of Spells was hidden somewhere on Tropal.

If he did not find it himself, then the boy would lead him to it. Whichever way, there would be destruction and chaos, death and darkness.

The children of Tropal were the key. As long as they breathed colour into the forest and gave it life, the Tree of Spells would remain hidden. Under his directions, the Drak were sent out to harvest the children, and to bring them to Black Mountain, where he imprisoned them in the dark, underground caves. Here, they lost their colours, and he drained them of all hope. They became soulless, devoid of emotions, and they lived the waking sleep – zombified.

He planned that he would set them to work and send them back out into the forest, like a virus, to touch and drain the colours; to kill every living plant and tree, every flower and blade of grass. Eventually, there wouldn't be enough healthy colours to keep the forest alive. Tropal would become a grey, dead Dimension, and the people would be his slaves.

Then, when he had the Tree of Spells, they would all become his unthinking, zombie army, his instruments of destruction, which he would use to conquer and drain the life force of the remaining Dimensions.

For now, he had to be patient. He could not leave his sanctuary. Daylight burnt and blistered his skin, and even the light of the moon blinded his eyes. He wallowed in the darkness of the caves, a darkness as black as the soil in a grave. He sent out the Drak to do his bidding, while he brooded and planned, waiting for his powers to strengthen, waiting for the moment when he would unleash a lightless shroud over Tropal, and claim the Tree of Spells as his prize.

He would be an unstoppable and invincible force. The Dimensions would be at his mercy. He would be free to conquer time and worlds beyond the Dimensions. The dark breath of his evil would touch every living thing, in all of space and time.

Recently, the warnings had come and he had felt an unwelcome tremor run through his body. Somewhere on Tropal, the force of the Chosen had been released, and as his skin crawled in revulsion, he sensed a connection with the individual who had unleashed it. In the cloying darkness, he smiled. Not a friendly, joyous smile, but one of evil anticipation.

'So,' he breathed deeply. 'You are here.'

With a flick of his glutinous tongue, he licked his earth-caked lips, and he thought of the boy Frog as nothing but a pestering, small insect, and he relished the anticipation of when he would squash him with one dismissive gesture.

6.

THE CRADLE

Frog stood between the Guardian and Mystra. The sign of the Chosen faded into her forehead and her colours now returned to the greens and browns of the forest. The Guardian had spoken quietly to her after she had survived her ordeal, and she now seemed calm and refreshed.

Frog had been bursting with questions and curiosity, but the Guardian counselled them both, advising them to have patience; they would talk more of the incident once they were in the Cradle.

They were standing in a small hut where, behind a screen, Frog had been allowed to wash himself with cool, refreshing water. The thick material of his medieval clothes was replaced with the lightweight wear of the forest people.

A green and brown, loose-fitting sleeveless top and a sort of kilt-style garment, which reached down to his knees, now adorned his wiry, but muscular frame. He still wore his short, leather boots. His sword was in its scabbard, and along with his pouch were both secured around his waist by a belt. The unseen talisman remained around his neck on its silver chain. His green 'Frog' clothes rested in a pile, the dragon-skin waistcoat folded, and his bullwhip coiled on top; they had felt cumbersome and awkward with his forest attire.

Mystra circled him, studying him until, with a nod of her head and a smile, she remarked, 'You'll do.'

Over the next few days, they would realise that she and Frog now had a bond, part of which was that she had inherited some of his personality, in particular his sense of humour.

The now familiar bird flew into the hut and alighted on the Guardian's shoulder. It trilled a soft melody, cocked its head sideways and flew off with the silence of a gentle breeze.

'Time to go,' announced the Guardian.

They made their way back to the trunk of the great tree and climbed another circular staircase, until they eventually emerged on to a wooden balcony. Stretching out in front of them was a rope walkway, which extended far above the forest floor. A meshwork of vines was strung along its length to prevent people from falling a great distance to the ground below. Frog tentatively looked down and quickly drew back before his eyes started to swim like apples in a barrel of water. He estimated that they were probably more than a hundred metres above the ground.

Suspended before them, there hung an enormous oval structure made of interwoven branches, vines and reeds.

'The Cradle,' announced the Guardian. 'Come, the Council will be waiting.'

He strode out along the narrow walkway, and Mystra prompted Frog to follow. His pride encouraged him to step into the Guardian's footsteps. He did not want to appear fearful, particularly in front of Mystra. He hid his fear, and keeping his eyes focussed on the saffron-robed figure in front of him, Frog journeyed out onto the gently swaying bridge.

'It's okay,' he quietly mumbled to himself. 'I'll probably die of a heart attack before I hit the ground!'

Finally, after a short while, but what seemed a lifetime to him, he stepped across the side of the Cradle, and with a quiet relief, down a few short steps and onto its floor. It was large enough to accommodate about fifty persons, and there was indeed a group of about half as many already assembled at its centre. It was with surprise that Frog realised they were all young people, who appeared to be in their teenage years. Each one of them wore a circlet of yew leaves on their heads. They were facing a small dais at one end, where the

Guardian had already positioned himself, and was now beckoning Frog to join him.

As he made his way to the platform, Frog noticed that around the edge of the Cradle, hundreds of small globes floated, as if defying gravity. The light that radiated from their misty interiors was tinged with orange. Small sparks of static seemed to play across their surface, and they glowed fiercely, even in the daylight.

Mystra joined the gathered group, one of whom placed a circlet of yew leaves upon her head. Frog took his place next to the Guardian, who stood perfectly still, looking out through a gap in the trees.

Frog thought that he had seen so many wonders, so many strange sights on his travels in the Dimensions, that nothing would surprise him anymore.

He was wrong!

He could, for the first time, see the purple-blue disc of the sun. A faint halo rippled around its edge as it hung, silhouetted against a pure white sky.

In a blink, it was replaced by a silver orbed moon, surrounded by a blanket of stardust diamonds, all looking as if they had been pasted onto a velvet black backdrop.

The Guardian turned Frog to face the young people standing in the Cradle.

'Behold. The Afterglow,' announced the Guardian.

All those gathered before him glowed as if under ultraviolet light. A shimmering iridescence, like the surface of soap bubbles caught in summer sunlight, reflected the spectrum of the rainbow across their bodies. Colours with such unseen depth and brightness reached out, and they washed over Frog like a transparent wave. He stood mesmerised, filled with feelings of sheer elation and astonishment as his clothes and his body rippled with a myriad of infinite colour.

He almost forgot to breathe.

Then, in the pulse of a heartbeat, it was gone. The Cradle and all who stood there were bathed in the orange, flickering lights of the globes.

As the Guardian took Frog's arm and led him down from the dais, the group formed a semi-circle and seated themselves on the floor, leaving a space for Frog and the Guardian to join them.

Twenty-five expectant faces turned in Frog's direction. He wasn't sure if they were waiting for him to say something, until at last, the Guardian spoke.

'Council of Tropal. We live in a troubled time. Of late, the evil one flexes his powers, and has begun his mission to destroy Tropal in his search for the Tree of Spells. I alone cannot stop him. As yet, I dare not confront him. I can use my powers only to defend and heal.'

Frog looked around at the young faces. Had

he heard right? That these twenty-five youngsters were the Council of Tropal?

'I present to you the Legend that is Frog,' declared the Guardian. 'He is the Chosen one. It is written that he is the one who above all can defeat the Dark Lord. It is he who has been charged with the task of stopping the Tree of Spells from falling into the hands of those who would destroy and enslave us all.'

Sitting there, listening to the Guardian speak, Frog felt a tiny crack open at the back of his mind, and the boy within him that was Chris, his true self, peeked through for a moment before melting back into the safety of his subconscious.

All of a sudden, Frog felt very small.

7.

THE TREE OF SPELLS

'Before the dawn of time,' continued the Guardian. 'There existed the one true magic. It is the lifeblood of everything.

'The Elements. Time. Birth. Life. Death. Body. Soul. Energy. Love. Hate. Good. Evil. It is everything that has been, everything that is, and everything that will be. Such is the power of this magic, that at a time on the edge of knowing, the first of the Guardians decided that not one individual should possess all of its workings and knowledge. Too dangerous was the responsibility; too awesome was the force that could destroy what was, what is, and what was meant to be.

'Magic is the living essence of seven powers –

Vita Aeterna:	One for Eternal Life
Absolute Scientia:	One for Absolute Knowledge
Potestatem Omnium:	One for Power over Others
Imperium Elementa:	One for Control over the Elements

Mortuos Suscitat:	One for the Ability to Raise the Dead
Anima Invicta:	One for an Invincible Soul
Imperium Tempus:	One for the Control of Time

'Many mages, sorcerers, wizards, witches, shamans and the like have acquired the power to command some of these spells, but none have owned them all. To do so would bring the end of ends! Such supremacy would corrupt even the meekest heart until eternal darkness, misery and evil would eventually triumph over all creation, and so each of the seven powers was transformed into the form of a single thing – the Tree of Spells.

'Only one living person has the ability to move the Tree of Spells without being tempted to use its powers. This is that person.'

The final statement made Frog start with self-recognition. He blinked as if waking from a dream. Twenty-five faces continued to stare at him, and this time he knew that it was his turn to speak.

'It's true,' he began hesitantly. 'I am the Frog of legend. I have faced Lord Mae—'

The Guardian placed a hand on Frog's arm. 'We do not speak his full name even in the haven of the Cradle. Remember that he senses all acknowledgement of his existence.'

'Sorry. I should have known by what happened to Mystra,' conceded Frog. 'I'll be more careful in future.' He turned back to address the group. 'I have faced him twice now and not put an end to him, even with the help of others. How I am to defeat him here, I am unsure. I hadn't even heard of the Tree of Spells until just before I arrived, and I haven't got a clue where to find it,' he admitted.

'Maybe this will help,' said the Guardian.

From his robes, he produced a small wooden box. Strange markings decorated its surface. It was very similar to the one that Gizmo, the Guardian of Castellion, had given to Frog, and as with that one, this box also had no visible way of opening it – no sign of hinges or a lid.

'This has remained in the keeping of the Guardians since time out of mind, and has been handed down through generations. Only you can open it.' He handed it to Frog.

Frog stared at the box. Now that he looked closer at it, he could have sworn that it was exactly like his own, the one that he had left wrapped up, hidden in the shed.

'Speak to it,' encouraged the Guardian. 'Whisper your name.'

Frog brought the box close to his lips and whispered, 'Frog.'

He had expected the top to melt open. Instead, the whole box evaporated into a fine mist, which dissolved into nothing. All that remained was a folded piece of tan-coloured material. It felt quite heavy in his hands as though it were some kind of animal skin. He also sensed that there was a small object wrapped in its folds. He tentatively unfolded it on his lap, to reveal lines of dark, ornate scripture etched into its surface. The object itself was a small, soapstone carving of a stern-looking face. It had deep inset eyes, an overlarge nose and pronounced lips. It resembled a miniature version of one of the Easter Island giant heads. The base of the figure was curved, so that no matter what you did, it would not stand up on a flat surface – it would just wobble and fall over.

There were hushed murmurs of excitement and fascination from the encircling group. Their body colours rippled with purples and soft blues of delight.

Frog turned the small figure over in his fingers. It felt smooth and somehow comforting to touch.

'May I?' asked the Guardian, and Frog passed it to him.

Frog turned his attention to the writing.

I am the first of four
Behind a silver screen
Where beasts roar
My place awaits me.
Let me sit to give you guidance.

'It's a riddle,' he announced. 'Why can't anyone just give plain directions?' he asked.

'Ah! Then life would be too simple, and what would life be without its challenges?' said the Guardian.

'A lot easier,' replied Frog, with a wry smile.

The Guardian turned to face Frog. 'In life, there are three types of people. Those who wait for things to happen; those who watch things happen; and finally, those who make things happen. Which one do you think you are?'

'I like to think that I make things happen,' replied Frog.

'That is why you will achieve so much in your life,' said the Guardian. 'That is why you were chosen.' He handed the stone figure and the script to Mystra. 'Pass these around. Perhaps amongst us, we can unravel this mystery.'

The group rose and gathered around Mystra, eager to inspect and touch the items.

'Will this lead us to the Tree of Spells?' asked Frog.

'I believe the first line says that this is indeed the

first of four clues, which, when put together with the others, will reveal the Tree of Spell's location.'

'Okay. Now that I've unlocked the first clue for you, why do you need me?'

'Because,' explained the Guardian. 'Others can be your eyes and ears, but they cannot fulfil the quest. It is you who must complete each task. Only you can take safe possession of the Tree of Spells.'

'What exactly do I do with it once I've found it?'

'You must take it into your world, and hide it in a place of the ancients, where it will never be found.'

Frog thought for a moment. 'Look. The Tree of Spells sounds pretty dangerous to me. You said that if one person had *all* of the powers, it could be the end of everything. So, when I find it, why don't you and the Guardians destroy it? End of problem.'

The Guardian nodded to himself and considered what Frog had said. 'To answer your question, let me ask you this. Firstly, do you believe in magic? Real magic?'

'If I didn't, then I wouldn't be here,' said Frog. 'Unless this is all a dream,' he added as an afterthought.

'I have already told you, the Tree of Spells is not just magic,' said the Guardian. 'Now. Look up to the sky.'

Frog gazed up through the canopy.

'What do you see?'

'A brilliant, silver moon, and loads of amazing stars.'

'Look closer. Do you see anything that you recognise?'

A familiar sight greeted Frog, as if all of the other stars in the sky had faded into the background.

'Orion's Belt!' Frog smiled.

'Where else have you seen these stars?'

Frog thought, his face upturned in wonder. 'In my own world, and also on Castellion and Aridian.'

'They exist across time, and in different Dimensions. So, are not all things connected?'

Frog wrinkled his nose. 'I guess so.'

'Whether we choose to believe in it or not, we are all connected by real magic,' said the Guardian. 'The Tree of Spells is the substance of *all* magic. The one who would possess it would have the power to extinguish even the stars. The Tree of Spells holds the very presence of magic together. If it ceased to exist, then so should we all. *That* is why we cannot destroy it.'

'And yet, you would trust me with it?'

'We must,' replied the Guardian. 'You are the Chosen one.'

'I just hope that I live up to your expectations.'

'I am sure that you will,' smiled the Guardian.

Frog turned his attention back to the Council, who were immersed in quiet conversation whilst they examined the writing and the small figurine.

'Why are they so young?' he asked. 'I would have expected that your Council would have consisted of people a lot older.'

'Ah!' A knowing smile passed over the Guardian's face. 'They may seem as though their ages are the same as yours, but for every one of your years, they have lived five. The members of the Council are gifted with the looks of eternal youth and longevity. They will live for more than two hundred of your years. It is as a result of the Afterglow.'

'Won't they ever look any older than they are now?' asked Frog.

'No. The power of the Afterglow keeps them looking youthful until the day that they pass on to the next life. Besides, you should know by now that things are not —'

Frog interjected. 'Always as they seem.' He smiled back at the Guardian. 'I remember when I was first told that; I don't suppose that you know how my old friend Gizmo is?'

'He is well. As is Castellion and its peoples.'

'Considering that there is such a time difference across the Dimensions,' said Frog, 'how long, in Castellion, has it been since I was there?'

'Less than ten of your years,' replied the Guardian.

'How come then, when I was on Aridian, the Guardian there told me that it had been a lot longer?' said Frog.

'Time ebbs and flows with the movement of the Slipstream. What will be tomorrow in Tropal can be yesterday in another Dimension,' explained the Guardian.

'Yet, in my world, time always stands still while I'm away.'

'As far as I understand,' the Guardian nodded.

'So, what about Aridian, and my friends there?'

'Many of your decades have passed since you walked their sands. I cannot reveal much to you, except that peace exists there still.'

'Why can't you tell me about my friends?'

The Guardian smiled gently at Frog. 'Because, a little knowledge can be a dangerous thing. Especially in the Dimensions.'

Their conversation was disturbed by a babble of discussion from Mystra and the group.

'We think that we know where this might be,' she said, as she indicated to the script.

'Go on,' said the Guardian.

'It is many days' walk from here,' she explained. 'To where the waters of the mighty Mandaran cascade with the sound of thunder, into the bottomless void, There is nowhere else like it on Tropal.'

'I know the place; the clue now brings it to mind,' agreed the Guardian. 'Well, my friend,' he said to Frog. 'It would appear that we have found the starting point for your quest. All that remains is to decide who from the Council shall accompany you.'

Twenty-five faces smiled eagerly at Frog.

'I think that *you* should choose those who should come along,' said Frog. 'Apart from yourself, of course.'

'I will not be travelling with you. I must stay with the community and face any threat that reaches here.'

'Typical Guardian.' Frog smiled, not unkindly. 'Throw me in at the deep end!'

Mystra stepped forwards and handed Frog the piece of material.

'I would be honoured to be your companion,' she said, with a warm smile. Her skin colour became a soft orange, like the first glow of a morning sun.

Memories of Fixer and Nadiah, his previous female companions from the other Dimensions, crept from the recesses of his mind. In that fleeting moment, he knew that he and Mystra's futures were destined to entwine.

'I will be honoured to have you as my companion and friend,' he replied. 'And I will trust your judgement on who should also join us.'

There was no undisciplined display of eagerness. No waving of hands and boisterous pleading. The group waited patiently for Mystra to speak. Her head moved from side to side as her eyes drifted across the Council.

'Jorge,' she announced.

A boy, roughly of Frog's stature, stepped forwards. Colours flowed and merged across his body. Mauves. Yellows. Blues. Greens; a palate of tints and friendly shades.

He smiled at Frog and gave the now familiar greeting of hands to head before he took his place next to Mystra. She continued to look at the faces for a moment, until she turned to the Guardian.

'I'm not sure,' she said.

He looked at the Council and asked, 'Who has the figure?'

A lean, tallish boy stepped forwards; his image reflected greens and browns. He held out his palm and the small statue rested gently there.

'Kal,' said the Guardian. 'You are the last companion. Take your place.'

As Kal joined Frog, Mystra and Jorge, Frog noticed that, unlike the others, Kal seemed to keep his colours under control. There was no flicker of pleasure, no display of delight.

The Guardian tapped his staff to the floor, and the globes swelled in their orange brilliance around the Cradle. 'Council of Tropal,' he announced. 'Behold the companions. Wish them well, for they take our future with them.'

8.

THE COMING OF THE GREY

An hour later, Frog, Mystra, Jorge, Kal and the Guardian were assembled together in the relative comfort of a small, circular hut.

Food and drink had been prepared, and they sat facing each other in the unsteady light of hanging lanterns. At the centre, an array of dishes was laid out, laden with fruits and meats. Small wooden bowls of freshly squeezed fruit juice were passed around.

Frog had learnt from past experience not to question the origin of the food, especially anything that looked like meat. He had adopted the motto of – 'If it looks and tastes good, then eat it.' Here, he recognised most of the familiar tropical fruits, which were bananas, mangos, coconut, and the like. He felt relaxed, and in particular, he had all but forgotten that the forest floor was many metres below him.

Mystra offered him a bowl of small, red berries, and as he took a handful, he could not help but hesitate and stare at the soft, earthy colours, which drifted like smoke across the back of her arm.

'Does it disturb you?' she asked.

'No. No,' he apologised.

'Touch my skin,' she said. 'Go on, touch it.' She offered her arm.

Frog stared; the expectation of physical contact skittered pleasantly across the inside of his stomach.

'What's the matter?' she asked. 'Too weird for you?' Her inherited sense of Frog's humour teased him.

He swallowed in anticipation and placed his index finger on her arm. His breath caught in his throat as her skin seemed to ripple in circles, like calm water after a pebble has been dropped into it. The colours did not change or merge, they simply undulated. Her arm felt no different than he thought that it would – soft and warm.

He became aware that everyone else was watching them, and he withdrew his hand.

'That would be a pretty neat trick if I could do it,' he said.

'I wonder,' said Mystra.

Frog's eyes followed her hand, and as if in slow motion, she reached out and placed her fingers on his arm. He had to blink several times as the subtle browns and greens of her skin melted like coloured water across his own. He felt the fine hairs stand up on the back of his neck as goose bumps surfaced in tiny pimples of exhilaration. The effect spread up past his elbow and he craned back his neck as it bled into the material of his sleeve. He panicked as he suddenly realised that he couldn't exhale, and black dots swam across his vision.

'Enough!' Mystra jerked back her hand as though she had received an electric shock. The sound of the Guardian's voice pumped Frog's lungs back into action and he breathed out and in; the fresh oxygen cleared his senses and brought light-headedness with it.

'He is not yet ready for such wonders,' said the Guardian. 'Who knows, he may never be the same should he be immersed fully into the transformation.'

Frog released a long sigh of relief as they all watched the effect fade and disappear from his skin

'I'm so sorry, Guardian,' murmured Mystra, with a bowed head.

'No. Really. It was my fault,' apologised Frog. *Maybe not one of my better ideas,* he thought.

'Let us concentrate on the matter at hand,' said the Guardian. 'At daybreak we shall all assemble here. I will arrange for travelling provisions to be prepared for your journey, which, I am sure, will be enough to take you well beyond Mandaran Falls. You will leave without ceremony or goodbyes. The Council has been pledged to secrecy, and the fewer who know of your whereabouts, the better. I have no doubt, young Frog, that the evil one will have knowledge of your presence here by now, and this will create more challenges for you as he reaches out with his growing powers.

'There will be much time for familiarity during your journey together, and I am sure that Jorge and Kal have many questions to ask of you. For now, I would propose that they tell you something about themselves. Let us first hear from Jorge.'

Over the next while, Frog heard of Jorge's exploits. Despite looking only fourteen, he had spent half of his life exploring Tropal and its history. It was he who had recognised the reference to Mandaran Falls in the riddle.

Kal, on the other hand, had always lived within the confines of the forest, as a tree shepherd, tending to the cultivation and health of all living plants.

Their conversation paused as it was interrupted by gentle tremors. A slight shudder sent miniature waves undulating across the surface of their drinks, and they all exchanged glances as if unsure of the sensation.

The Guardian stood. He gripped his staff with both hands, and planted it into the matting of the floor. As Frog watched, the staff began to quiver. The vibration grew, until it looked as though the Guardian were using all of his strength to hold the staff in place.

'Lie down!' he shouted. 'Lie down and hold on to each other.'

Such was the urgency in his voice that no one questioned him. No sooner had they spread out on the floor, arms gripping arms, when the shockwave hit them. The hut creaked and groaned with movement. The very air around them vibrated. It was as if the hut had been wrenched from its secure place amongst the trees, and was tossed like a leaf in the wind. It felt as though the hand of a hurricane had picked it up and shaken it like a moneybox, searching for loose coins.

As with most frightening moments, what was the passing of only a few seconds appeared to be a timeless horror.

With one dull, muffled explosion, more felt than heard, there came a silence. When the tempest stopped, they lay entangled with each other, shaken but unharmed. Emptied bowls and spilt food lay strewn around like discarded rubbish. A section of the roof hung open like an attic door.

The Guardian stood firm and unmoved.

'Are you all alright?' he asked. His voice was calm and unhurried.

They stood cautiously, flexing their arms and legs, checking themselves for injuries.

'I think that we're okay,' said Frog. He looked around at the others. 'What was that? An earthquake?'

'It was not of nature's making,' replied the Guardian. 'Follow me, all of you, and stay close.'

Outside of the hut, they could see more activity and damage. A few lanterns had set fire to a number of huts, and chains of people, wielding buckets of water, were already dousing them under control. A walkway had collapsed, and hung twisted and broken as it dangled precariously above the forest floor.

A small figure came running along from another walkway, and Frog recognised the girl as a member of the Council. Her distress was visible by the subdued, flickering colours on her skin.

'One of the Great Trees has fallen,' she announced, her eyes moist with tears.

'Show me,' said the Guardian.

Frog, Mystra, Jorge and Kal trailed behind the Guardian, who strode after the scurrying footsteps of the girl.

She led them along connecting platforms, then out across a number of suspended walkways. Frog was thankful that he could only catch glimpses of the ground far below through the thick foliage. Even so, it took all of his concentration to cope with the swaying motion of the walkways as they urgently crossed them.

As they journeyed, he became truly aware of the extent of the Canopy as it spread out in all directions, above and below them; it was in reality the size of a small town, constructed in the trees.

It took them a good ten minutes of travelling along a myriad of walkways before Frog became aware of a low humming noise. It reached his ears as a soft drone.

They alighted onto a large, circular platform, and Frog realised that the sound was of voices; a wailing of sorrowful harmonies was coming from a large crowd of people who were gathered there. They parted to let the Guardian and the girl through, and Frog and the others followed. The girl raised her arm and pointed ahead to a collapsed walkway. Her tear-stained cheeks faced the Guardian as she said with a trembling voice – 'There.'

They moved forwards until they came to a halt at a safe distance from the jagged and splintered edge of a platform that looked as though it had been ripped away in rage and anger. The tangled remains of half the walkway hung down unsteadily from above them. At first, Frog could not discern anything else untoward, until in the flickering lights of lanterns and torches, his eyes focussed on an enormous dark space ahead of them.

'What's happened?' he asked.

Without a reply, the Guardian tapped the base of his staff on the floor, and the globe set into its top began to radiate a soft, yellow glow. He passed his hand over the light, and then unfolded his fingers to reveal half a dozen small, but very bright lights, like fireflies, which nestled on his palm, and he gently blew across them. The lights floated out like sprites on the wind, to hover over the scene and illuminate the devastation below.

The trunk and branches of a great tree lay felled

across the forest floor, its enormous roots gouged up out of the earth like a tangle of broken limbs. Its trunk and branches were split open, and the once vibrant green leaves were now grey and lifeless as was all of the forest around it and beyond. What were once beautiful, colour-rich flowers was now a carpet of monotone grey.

Kal was the first to spot the lifeless form that lay amongst the devastation.

With a mournful groan, he held out both of his hands in its direction. Overcome with emotion, he sank to his knees, sobbing as the colours of his skin flickered with sickly greens and yellows, and his shoulders shook with grief.

'Who is it?' asked Frog.

'His brother, and my closest friend,' said Jorge, who's own complexion had turned pale and ashen.

'Another innocent instrument of the evil one's merciless ambitions,' said the Guardian. He turned, and Frog could see the Guardian's calm countenance had been replaced with grim resolve. 'Jorge, take Kal to be comforted by his family, and then summon the rest of the Council to gather in the Cradle. Wait for us there. Frog, Mystra, come with me. Our skills are needed on the forest floor.'

Frog endured a nerve-wracking journey down to the ground, in what he now considered in his own mind was just a flimsy hanging basket. With his feet firmly on the floor, he closely followed the others through the wrecked and twisted shrubbery. They moved purposefully and carefully over and around broken boughs and sections of fallen walkways, until they reached the upturned base of the tree. A massive hole of churned-up earth was left behind by the torn-out roots, which towered over them as if they clawed at the sky.

They worked their way around the tangled disorder, until with his outstretched arms; the Guardian brought them to a halt. Just ahead, it was as though an invisible line had been drawn, and everything beyond it was devoid of colour. He planted the base of his staff just in front of his feet and into the sickly, grey debris. Frog watched, as at first a glimmer of pale green washed slowly out like a pool of gently flowing liquid. As it spread out, the colour bled into the ground and created a healthy corridor for them to walk along.

'Do not stray from the colour,' he said, and holding the staff before him, he stepped forwards, and they hesitantly followed on behind.

Moving around split and splintered branches, they reached an enormous fallen bough, which blocked their way. The lifeless grey body of a young boy lay propped against it. The spreading, pale green from the Guardian's staff lapped in gentle waves around the limp form, but had no effect on it.

'Is he…?' Frog did not want to utter the word.

'Give me one of the leaves. Quickly!' instructed the Guardian.

Frog opened his pouch and held out a silver-green frond. The Guardian crouched down and gently placed it in the boy's mouth, and as they watched, it dissolved on his tongue.

'Mystra, come here,' beckoned the Guardian.

Mystra knelt beside the Guardian; her eyes were tearful. 'His name is Gabe. He disappeared about a month ago. Taken by the Drak,' she said to Frog, her voice a cracked whisper.

The Guardian took her hand and guided it to the boy's forehead.

'Trust me,' he smiled.

Frog stood there, and he watched with wonder as the golden glow of the Chosen filtered out from Mystra's palm and onto the boy's face. It brought back memories to him of how he had used the same power to restore his friend Billy Smart back to life, in another place and time.

The radiance flowed through the boy's body, until it completely enveloped him.

'Enough,' said the Guardian, and he lifted Mystra's hand away. 'You have saved his body; now let us pray that his mind has also survived.'

They watched the radiance fade as his skin took on the soft mixture of healthy blues and greens. The boy's chest rose and fell with the soft rhythm of steady breathing – it was Frog who found himself holding his own breath as he waited for the boy to open his eyes.

With the fluttering movement of a butterfly's wings, the boy's eyelids lifted to reveal clear, aquamarine eyes. He brought up a hand and brushed back a dark lock of his hair that had fallen across his brow. Uncertain, he looked at each one of them in turn, his eyes finally coming to rest on Frog.

'Do I know you?' he asked, as if trying to recall a distant memory.

'He is a friend, come to aid us,' said the Guardian, and he helped the boy to sit up.

'I sense that he is more than that,' said the boy. 'I feel that I should know his name. It sits at the back of my throat, waiting to be said.' He leant on the Guardian and got unsteadily to his feet to face Mystra and give her the now familiar greeting with his hands on his forehead. 'Thank you, Mystra, for the gift that you have given me.' He turned and gave the same gesture to Frog. 'I am Gabe. Thank you for bringing me back from the dark.'

'It was Mystra who healed you,' said Frog.

'I sense that the power came from you also,' said Gabe. 'We are, in some way...' He hesitated. 'Connected.'

Frog felt the stirring of an unseen bond with Gabe. It tickled the back of his memory like an old friend. 'My name is...'

'Frog.' Gabe smiled.

9.

LET THE LIGHT...

When they returned to the top level of the Canopy, small groups were already busy working away, lifting and removing debris whilst others were starting to repair the damaged areas.

The Guardian turned to Gabe. 'Go to your brother, give him hope and strength.'

Gabe looked at Frog. 'I hope that we will meet again.'

'I'm sure that we will,' replied Frog, with a smile.

As Gabe scampered off along a walkway, the Guardian took Frog and Mystra straight to the Cradle, where Jorge was waiting with the assembled Council. The Guardian signalled for the three of them to stand on the dais with him.

'The Dark Lord touches the very roots of the Canopy,' he announced. 'He sends lost children of Tropal as his unseeing slaves to extinguish the colours and to test our resolve. I know that he is not yet strong enough to overcome us, but we must protect ourselves and prepare for the worst. I will stay here and use my powers as a Guardian to defend the Canopy. Now, only Mystra and Jorge shall accompany Frog on his quest. I have decided that Kal will not be travelling as a companion.'

Mystra and Jorge exchanged a glance of surprise.

'The hour is late,' continued the Guardian. 'Let us try to bring a restful night to the community.'

The Guardian waited for the Council to disperse, before he led the companions back to a large hut. Around the walls were three low wooden bunks, and placed on each one was what looked like to Frog three small, leather backpacks.

'I have arranged for some of your personal items to be brought here,' said the Guardian.

Frog looked on as the others rummaged through their packs, eagerly checking the contents. 'I feel slightly underprepared,' he said.

'There are a few provisions and a water bottle in your pack for you,' said the Guardian.

'Where are my other clothes?' asked Frog.

'Not to worry, I have them in safekeeping for you,' replied the Guardian.

Frog noticed that Mystra and Jorge each had a wooden tube placed on their bunks. Intrigued, he picked up Jorge's and inspected it. He slowly turned it over in his hands; it was lighter than he expected, and the texture of the wood was smooth to his touch. It was about sixty centimetres in length and had a hole at one end. Fixed over the other end was a piece of leather with a small slit in it.

'Have you used one before?' asked Jorge.

'I don't even know what it is,' admitted Frog.

'A blowpipe,' said Jorge. 'We use them mainly for hunting,' he explained.

'And competitions,' added Mystra.

'Mystra is Tropal's champion, but one day, I'll beat her,' said Jorge, with a smile.

'In your dreams,' Mystra teased.

'Enough talk for now. You must rest,' interrupted the Guardian.

After settling into their bunks, despite the evening's events, they all benefitted from a dreamless sleep until the Guardian roused them a few hours later. When they had eaten a light breakfast, they slung their leather packs across their backs, and made their way down to the forest floor.

Just as the darkness blinked into daylight, so they stood, momentarily adjusting their eyes as the purple-blue disc appeared in the sky and filtered shifting spots of light through the Canopy.

The Guardian turned to Jorge. 'I sense that something troubles you.'

'I just don't understand why only three of us. Could not Gabe have taken Kal's place?'

'Gabe was not destined to take part in the quest, and Kal's resolve would not have been strong enough for the challenges ahead.'

'How do you know that I will be strong enough?'

The Guardian raised an eyebrow. 'I do not need to know; only you will answer that.' He looked at the three companions. 'There is much mystery in our lives, most of which is revealed only when we least expect it.' He placed his staff upright in front of him, and as he stepped back it remained standing, unaided. 'Join your hands around it.'

They clasped hands, and each one exchanged a nervous, expectant look with the others. A soft yellow glow returned to the globe, and three veins of golden static reached out and touched the foreheads of Frog, Mystra, and a wide-eyed Jorge. The sign of the Chosen radiated on each of their brows, and their hair and clothes billowed out as an unseen wind danced around them.

'Let the Light deliver us from evil,' said the Guardian.

'Let the Light deliver us from evil,' they repeated with one voice.

With one final gust, the wind passed over them, and then all was still.

'The circle is complete,' announced the Guardian.

We are here. Three voices echoed gently in Frog's head.

Whilst he was in Castellion, he had been given the ability to hear the thoughts of any of the other Chosen, but this was different. He did not only hear the words; he sort of saw them in the back of his head, a bit like mental texting, which was accompanied by a cloudy image of those who were sending the message.

He turned and smiled at Mystra and Jorge. *Hi*, he thought. They smiled back.

The Guardian did not utter a sound, but his words drifted into their heads. *Use this gift with great care. Its power diminishes over distance, and it is not immune to the prying thoughts of the evil one. There is no doubt that he will grow in strength, and you must learn to shield yourselves. Find the Tree of Spells, and restore balance to the Dimensions. Now, go.*

Without another spoken word, the three companions bowed a farewell to the Guardian. They turned and silently made their way along a small forest path, and with them went Tropal's unknown destiny and the future of the Dimensions.

10.

MANDARAN FALLS

Jorge led the way; it seemed natural that he should lead, as he was the most travelled amongst them. He knew as much, if not more than the Guardian, of Tropal's landscape and topography.

As they walked, the sounds of the forest echoed around them. Nothing seemed to clash in discord. The birdsong, the call of hidden creatures, even the movement of the leaves seemed to be in harmony.

Three days passed without incident as they trekked through dappled groves and along pleasant pathways. Their nights were spent sleeping under a blanket of stars and to the soft thrumming of the forest. They encouraged Frog to tell them of his adventures in Castellion and Aridian, and they sat enthralled as he spoke of dragons, Ice People and Sandspiders. However, he took heed of the Guardian's warning, and no matter how much they pleaded with him, he disclosed no details of his own Dimension or of his life there.

During the afternoon of the fourth day, Frog became aware of a deeper sound, which at first seemed to vibrate softly through the air, but as they journeyed on, the ground began to tremble beneath their feet, until the noise rose to a rushing and rumbling like that of a restless summer storm.

Jorge turned, and with a smile, ended Frog's concerns. 'Mandaran!' he said.

His colours rippled with excitement and he quickened his pace, pushing aside fern fronds as he went. Frog and Mystra trotted along behind him like a little train of excited toddlers. The temperature dropped a few degrees as a fine mist filled the air, and moisture dripped lazily from the surrounding foliage. The noise reached a crescendo, and they pushed through a final barrier of vegetation, to be drenched in deafening clouds of spray, which rose up from white depths of thunder, countless metres below them.

They were on a wide precipice, looking across to a point where the endless torrent of a great churning river cascaded in the sunlight like a rolling silver-grey curtain, which fell down into a watery oblivion, from where shimmering rainbows arced out of the billowing mist. Frog reached inside his pouch and brought out the piece of material with the clue written on it. He studied it again, particularly the second line –

Behind a silver screen.

He looked back at the cascading torrent. Mystra leaned forwards and her words appeared in his head.

No doubt about it. We have to find a way to get behind the falls.

'Jorge. Have you been behind the falls before?' shouted Frog.

'No,' he hollered back. 'But there's a first time for everything! Follow me; we need to find a path.'

He turned and pushed his way into the undergrowth. They shuffled along behind him with their hair and clothing clinging wetly to their bodies.

After a few moments, he brought them to a halt. 'We've got two choices,' he shouted. 'We can either back-track into the forest and hope to pick up another trail that will take us down to the falls, or we could take a chance and make our way along the side of the gorge.'

For a moment, they stood there, undecided, and then Frog spoke up. 'Did anyone bring any rope?'

'What for?' asked Jorge.

'Well, if we roped ourselves together, like mountaineers, then it wouldn't be so dangerous climbing down the rocks,' he explained.

'Mountain ears?' asked Jorge, a frown on his face.

'Sorry,' Frog laughed. 'Where I come from,

mountaineers are what we call people who climb mountains.'

They looked at Frog as though they expected more information from him.

'It doesn't matter,' he said. 'Ropes will just make things safer for us, in case someone slips.'

'Ah!' exclaimed Jorge. 'I'll be back in a bit.'

He turned and disappeared into the undergrowth. Within a couple of minutes, he was back, trailing a long length of thick, sturdy vine behind him.

'Rope,' he said, with a big, satisfied smile.

Having linked themselves together, they made their way towards the edge of the cliff. All three of them peered over and looked down into the swirling mixture of spray and mist. Far below, at the base of the rock face, great flat slabs of wet stone appeared to be the beginnings of a rough walkway.

Frog signalled for them to clasp their hands over their ears to smother as much of the noise out as possible. Next, they crouched in a circle and pushed their heads together.

Frog used his thoughts. *If you can get another long length of vine, we should be able to abseil down.*

Abseil? echoed Mystra and Jorge.

Frog looked at the confused expressions on their faces.

Okay. He breathed in. *I guess that it will be easier if I show you.*

Frog's memories took him back his own

Dimension, to the previous summer and his Duke of Edinburgh outward-bound week. One of the activities that he had been introduced to and enjoyed so much was orienteering and abseiling. His instructor had dubbed him 'a natural'. Of course, Frog recalled, that was with all of the safety gear and the right equipment. Here, all he had to stop him falling to his death was a length of forest vine and the strength of his new friends!

He started to untie himself.

'What are you doing?' Jorge had decided that it was easier to shout.

Frog shouted back. 'Go and get a really long piece of vine, long enough to reach from here to the bottom of the cliff.'

Jorge took one more look over the edge then turned to go.

'Oh, by the way, make sure that it's strong enough to take my weight,' Frog added, just to be sure.

When Jorge returned, he brought exactly what Frog had asked for, and after looping the vine around a tree, Frog tied one end around his waist, and threw the other over the edge, to trail down like a limp, green snake.

Frog shouted slowly; he didn't want any misunderstanding. 'You have to hold on to the vine and lower me down gradually. When I reach the bottom, I'll untie myself and you can pull the vine back up for the next person. They'll have the added security that I'll be hanging on to this end as well.'

Jorge took a step closer to the edge and peered nervously down.

'Suddenly, I vote for the long way around,' he said. His colours seemed to thin and pale.

'Then I'll already be down there waiting for you,' said Frog. 'Now take the strain because I'm going.'

They grasped the vine as Frog moved himself backwards and out over the edge. Steadily, he disappeared into the swirling cloud of vapour.

They heard his voice in their heads. *Keep it coming. Slowly. Slowly.*

Afterwards, he had to admit that he enjoyed it with a reckless, nervous energy, mainly because he couldn't see a thing due to the moisture soaking his face and running into his eyes.

Mystra came next; her determination to be as skilful as Frog overcame her initial dread, so that by the time she landed on her feet at Frog's side, she was grinning like a Cheshire cat, her skin rippled with reds and blues of pleasure.

Jorge had elected to come last; however, at one point his panic resulted in him tangling himself in the vine, so that for a while he hung there like a helpless marionette. Thankfully, he was only a couple of metres away from the bottom when this happened. Nevertheless, Frog still took a precarious climb up to him to calm him and untangle the vine, before helping him the rest of the way down to join Mystra.

When they were safely together again, Jorge cut a long length of the vine, coiled it and slung it over his shoulder.

'It could come in handy,' he explained.

The drenched and sodden group set off along the rock path towards the heart of the falls. The sound was deafening now, and none of them tried to communicate with each other unless with sign language and gestures.

The force of the cascading torrent vibrated up through the layers of solid rock and into their bones. Sharp needles of spray flew at them and stung their skin, like a swarm of annoyed gnats, and they shielded their eyes as they struggled on. The rocky platform had now become so narrow that they shuffled along sideways with their backs pressed against the rock face. The moisture had become so dense that breathing was an effort. They gasped as their lungs struggled to filter out any oxygen, and they were in danger of suffocating, drowning in the waterlogged air. Frog was about to signal that they should turn back and look for another route, when Jorge tugged at his arm and excitedly indicated towards a dark shape in the mist ahead. As they got closer, they could see that it was a rough archway, carved into the rock. Frog signalled to Mystra who nodded back with a sense of urgency.

With a frantic determination, they stumbled into a small cave, and dropped to their hands and knees with exhaustion. They desperately sucked in the clear air; their chests heaved with the effort until slowly their breathing returned to normal. As they sat there, regaining their strength; Frog was the first to speak.

'Listen.'

The others cocked their heads and glanced around them.

'What?' asked Mystra.

'It's quiet,' pointed out Frog.

The air was filled with a gentle, distant hum, even though only a metre or so away the tumbling torrent cascaded a curtain of spray across the mouth of the entrance.

'My hair's tingling,' said Jorge. He ran his fingers through the long, lank strands.

'It feels weird,' agreed Mystra, as she tentatively pulled at one of her locks.

They all stood, uneasy of the sensation that they were feeling. To their amazement, and slowly at first, droplets of water from their heads floated out into the air around them. Then the liquid that soaked their clothes and belongings began to separate and drift out to form globules of water, which hovered above them. Even the wet puddles fed by their dripping garments, which had gathered on the floor around them, floated up in water-filled bubbles.

Mystra held her arms out and looked at her clothes in wonder. 'I'm nearly dry!' she exclaimed.

Within the next few moments, every drop of moisture was removed from them, to hang, unaffected by gravity, over their heads like a cloud of bubble-wrap. Then, as if attracted by magnetism, it stretched out towards the entrance, before it disappeared into the mist outside.

'Well. That was interesting,' said Frog.

11.

WATER

The cave was lit by a silver-grey light, which filtered in through the way that they had entered. Almost opposite, there was another archway, and the same light illuminated beyond that. There was no other exit, and so, with Jorge leading the way, they stepped through it.

There should have been a deafening, ear-splitting, thunderous noise. Instead, there was just a quiet, steady 'siiisss' – a sound very much like bacon sizzling gently in a pan.

Now, they stood behind the base of the falls; a wall of liquid fury fell endlessly in front of them as they faced an enormous, bubbling white curtain.

Mystra held out her hand. 'Look. There's no spray. Not a drop of water is falling inside of the cave.'

To Frog and Jorge's astonishment, she calmly stuck her hand into the torrent. 'It tickles,' she announced, before she withdrew it to inspect her palm. She held it up for the others to see. 'It's perfectly dry,' she smiled.

'You idiot!' said Frog. 'You could have been pulled in. We could have lost you.'

She gave him a cheeky grin. 'But I wasn't,' she replied, as ripples of orange and butter-yellow ran across her skin.

Frog was about to argue with her further, when Jorge spoke up. He was staring at what was behind them.

'Is everyone feeling energetic?' he asked.

The others turned to follow his gaze.

A stone stairway was cut into the wall of the cave, and it zigzagged its way to where a small platform of rock jutted out, nearly thirty metres above them. Set back from this was another archway.

As their eyes followed the line of steps, their necks craned back, and each one of them tried to mentally calculate how many there were.

'Must be at least five hundred,' said Jorge.

'More like a thousand' groaned Frog.

'It doesn't make any difference,' said Mystra. 'Look at that dark patch, about halfway up.'

Their eyes followed the direction of her pointing finger. What at first glance seemed to be a shadow on the stairway was in fact a large, broken gap. Seemingly, sometime in the not too recent past the rock had collapsed and taken several of the steps with it. Frog's eyes followed the cave wall down to the floor, and slightly puzzled, he noticed that there was an absence of rubble or broken stones lying there.

'There's got to be another way,' said Jorge, as he looked around the cave. 'Another doorway or passage,' he said hopefully. 'Everybody split up and search.'

There were several shadowed recesses around the cave, but none led to any other exit. Frog had just squeezed out of a narrow dead end, when he heard an excited Mystra calling them.

She stood in a corner of the cave with the elusive platform and archway high above them, and they gathered around her,

'It's fantastic,' she announced.

'Amazing,' said Jorge.

'Weird,' mused Frog. He stood mesmerised, looking at what should have been impossible.

Water trickled out of a crack in the rock and splashed into a natural stone bowl, which was full to the brim. The water then dripped steadily over the edge to continue on its journey. In any normal circumstances, to find a small spring in a cave would not be out of the ordinary; however, this one flowed upwards!

The water came out of the hole and ran up into an upside-down basin. It collected there in a little pool, against the laws of gravity. The water trickled over the edge, and ran in a thin silvery stream of liquid all the way up to the cave's ceiling, where it collected like a mercurial puddle. The thin watery veins trickled across the roof above the platform and away through the archway.

'I didn't touch anything,' she explained. 'I was just standing here, and it suddenly started to flow.'

They stood there in silence, fascinated by the phenomenon until Jorge spoke.

'Here's a thought. Do you think that if we soaked ourselves in the water, we would float up to the platform?'

'It's worth a try,' said Frog, excitedly.

Mystra stepped back and looked at the height of the rock overhang. 'Hold on,' she said, nervously. 'What if it isn't enough to get us right to the top? What if we stop halfway up?'

'Tell you what,' said Jorge. 'I'll go first.' He uncoiled the vine from his shoulder. 'You can tie one end of this to my ankle and you can pull me back down with it if I get stuck.'

'It might not be long enough to reach all the way,' said Frog.

'Then I'll have to climb back down, won't I?' Jorge argued.

They could see the determination on his face as he knelt down and tied one end of the vine to his leg. When he was happy that it was secure enough, he stood up.

'Right. Splash as much of the water on me as you

can, and don't let me float up until I'm absolutely soaked.'

They cupped their hands and scooped water from the upside-down bowl, which was not as easy to do as they had thought. The biggest problem was that as soon as they threw the water at Jorge, it just floated away towards the ceiling, before it even touched him. No matter how they tried, every drop of liquid skittered away skyward, like a disobedient chemistry experiment.

'Impossible!' Jorge shook his head in frustration.

'I've got another idea,' said Frog. 'But it's a bit risky.'

'What can be riskier than what we've tried?' Mystra shrugged.

'What do you think would happen if we actually drank the water?' he asked.

'You're right. It is riskier,' said Jorge. 'And crazy!' He added for good measure.

'Call me crazy, then,' said Frog. He stepped forwards and closed his mouth over a thin stream of water. He filled his mouth with it, stood back and swallowed with two gulps.

The others looked at him with a mixture of amazement and curiosity.

'Well?' asked Mystra. 'What does it taste like?'

'Nothing,' said Frog. 'But I do feel a little light-headed.'

They stared at him.

'It's a joke,' Frog explained.

They continued to stare at him.

'I said it was a joke! Sorry if you don't find it funny,' he said.

'No. It's not that,' said Jorge. 'Look at your feet!'

Frog looked down. He was floating. Only a few centimetres from the ground, but he was definitely floating.

'It's working! Quick, let me drink some more.'

Frog leant forwards once again and gulped down three more mouthfuls. He could feel his body becoming lighter. There was a tingling sensation in his stomach, as though it was full of popping candy.

'Don't drink too much,' warned Jorge. 'Or you'll have trouble getting down. You don't know how long the effect will last.'

'Hang on to me. Quickly!'

He took another three gulps. He could see the material of his clothes straining to be released from Jorge and Mystra's grip. His feet were now well off the floor.

'I guess that it's the moment of truth,' he said. 'Let me go.'

They released him and he rose away from them with the lazy speed of a tired helium balloon. Unfortunately, he was well out of their reach when Jorge shouted up.

'Sorry. In all of the excitement, I forgot to tie this on you.' He held up the limp end of the vine.

Frog looked down as he floated higher and higher, rising amongst the thin streams of liquid. He was halfway up, when a fearless thought crept into his head. *Eat your heart out, David Blaine!*

It was quickly followed by a thought from Mystra. *Who's David Blaine?*

Just some illusionist guy from my Dimension who I think would be impressed, he thought back.

Jorge's voice came into his head. *Never mind that, you're not far off now. You need to slow down.*

Frog looked up. The glistening pool of water and the ceiling was a few metres above him, and he reached out to grab at the platform as he approached it. The rough edge touched his hand and he grasped at the rock; his fingers found a hold and he pulled himself across the ledge. There were a couple of old, large metal rings set into the wall, and he grabbed at one of them. His body gently bobbed like a ball caught on a wave, as he steadied himself with the aid of the ring.

I've made it, he thought out to the others. *It's a bit of a weird sensation, but nothing unpleasant. Decide who wants to come up next, and drink six mouthfuls of the water, no more, no less.*

A few minutes later, he was pleasantly surprised to see two smiling faces rising gently above the edge of the platform, their shapes flickering in a myriad of pleasant colours. They scrabbled forwards and he helped them to cling to the large metal rings.

Eventually they floated in a row, horizontally, with their legs trailing out behind them.

'Wow!' Mystra smiled. 'That was fun!'

'Ouch!' said Jorge as he bumped the side of his head.

'Once you get used to it,' said Frog, 'it's a bit like swimming.'

'I don't usually bump my head when I go swimming,' complained Jorge.

'I wonder how long this is going to last for?' said Mystra.

'I guess as long as it remains in our bodies,' said Frog.

'You mean, until we have to…?' said Jorge. 'Oh! I don't even want to think about how that's going to turn out!'

12.

THE FLOATING STAIRCASE

Following a short discussion, they had agreed to use their temporary skill to an advantage, and after linking themselves together with the vine, and with Frog leading the way; they floated through the stone archway and along a narrow passageway.

Jorge still had problems controlling his direction, and he kept bumping into Mystra. Some people suffer from negative buoyancy and find it hard to swim; Frog felt that in Jorge's case he suffered from negative gravity, and found it hard to float!

'We're losing light,' Jorge pointed out, as they reached a curve in the tunnel.

Sure enough, the light that reached them from the waterfall was not strong enough to radiate further into the passage. Frog peered around the bend and into darkness.

'Torches,' he complained. 'We should have brought torches.'

'I'm sorry,' interrupted Mystra. 'But I need to go.'

'Go where?' asked Jorge.

'You know. *Go!*' emphasised Mystra.

Jorge's face turned crimson red with embarrassment.

'Wait here,' she told them as she untied herself.

With little effort, she floated around the corner and into the darkness, whilst the others hovered awkwardly with their own silent thoughts.

After a few minutes, she emerged smiling, and walking on her feet. 'You'll be pleased to know that everything's normal, and it doesn't run out upwards.'

'Oh. That is so gross! I really did not want that image in my head,' said Frog.

Jorge quickly untied himself and bounced past Mystra. 'Sorry, but I've got to go now too.'

In the end, even Frog took the opportunity to relieve himself in the darkness, until eventually back in the shadowed tunnel, they stood as a group, the gravity-defying effect of the water now gone.

'So, now what?' asked Jorge. 'We're still stuck.'

'Well, we can't go back,' said Frog. 'So we've no option but to follow the passage.'

'We don't know how long it goes on for, or what danger there might be in the darkness,' said Jorge. 'There could be a hidden drop into a bottomless pit. Or we may become lost and never find our way out.'

'Thanks for being so cheerful,' said Frog.

'Just saying,' replied Jorge, apologetically.

'I think that it's a test,' said Frog.

'What do you mean?' asked Mystra.

'I have a feeling that it's testing me to see if I'm the right person to discover the Tree of Spells. It's a series of challenges designed to protect the clue.' He made an instant decision. 'Tie the rope to me; I'll walk along slowly to see where the passage leads. If I get into trouble, you can pull me back.'

Frog found himself inching his way along in the dark, with one hand on the cold rock wall and the other stretched out before him. He stumbled along like a blind man who has lost his cane. The darkness was absolute; it clung to him like a shroud. He couldn't even see himself blink.

His hand found the rough edge of a corner and he eased himself around it. That was when his foot struck the base of a step.

'I seem to be at the bottom of a flight of steps,' he shouted. His words sounded dull and toneless as the blackness swallowed them up. There was no answer from the others. He shouted out again, this time louder. There was still no response.

He used his thoughts. *Mystra. Jorge. Do you hear me?*

To his relief, there came two responses. *Yes. Yes.*

Did you not hear me shouting?

Jorge. *When?*

Just now. Twice.

Not a sound, Jorge replied.

Strange. How much vine is there left?

Jorge. *Not much.*

I'm at the foot of a flight of steps. It's still pitch black, but I'm going to take a chance and climb them.

He lifted his foot, but found nothing. There was no second step! He crouched down and slid his hand across the surface of the first step. The stone was rough as though newly hewn. He pushed his fingers forwards. Where the face of the next tread should be, there was a gap, an empty space; his hand moved forwards into nothing, a void.

Now why would anyone build just one step? he wondered to himself.

In his mind, he tried to visualise what was before him in the darkness. *One step, then nothing. One step, then nothing,* he repeated.

Mystra's voice came to him. *What's further up?*

What do you mean?

Is it just a large gap? Is the next one higher?

He inched forwards, and brought his hand up to where a third step might be.

She was right! There was something there! His palm pressed against cold stone and he moved his hand up to feel the rough ridge and flat surface of another footstep.

You're right! Slacken the vine; I'm going to see if there is another one further up.

He felt the tension on the vine relax, and he

moved forwards to position himself onto the first unseen step. The third step was about waist high, and he pulled himself up to bring his body onto it. It moved! In fact, it was more like a wobble. He froze as his legs swung underneath it into nothing. In his panic, the darkness seemed to smother him.

'It's just a test. It's just a test,' he repeated to himself out loud.

He hauled his body onto what he could now feel was another slab of stone, about a metre wide and roughly sixty centimetres deep. It rocked and tilted as though suspended in mid-air. The vine tightened and threatened to pull him back down into the unknown void.

Stop! Don't pull the vine! 'Stop! Don't pull the vine!' he thought and shouted out at the same time.

Jorge's voice came into his head. *What's happening?*

The steps are spaced really wide apart, and they move. I could tip myself off if I'm not careful. I'm going to see how far up they go. How much more of the vine is there?

That's it. I'm holding the end, Jorge replied.

I'll just have to take a chance. Let it go.

Back down the passage, Jorge let go of the vine, and together, he and Mystra watched it slither away into the darkness, as if it had a life of its own.

Frog steadied himself on his knees and let the stone settle beneath him before he attempted to ease his body up to the next step. This proved to be trickier, because as he transferred his weight from one step to the other, they both moved, not drastically, but enough to unnerve him. His mind became focussed on the perilous gaps rather than the unstable steps. It took all of his concentration to complete the next movement upwards. He was on a floating stairway above what could be a bottomless crevasse, and he couldn't see a thing!

Time seemed to flow unhurriedly, stretching itself out like sticky treacle. When he had slowly eased himself up ten of the wobbling stone platforms, he noticed a sliver of grey light above him. This gave him confidence and he pressed on. As he progressed, the source of the light formed the shape of a closed door; it escaped through the edges of the doorframe as if to tease him of what was beyond.

He shifted upwards, step by step, and the detail of the stairway became more visible, but so too did the darkness on which it, and he, floated. Emptiness stretched out on either side, above and below him into an inky blackness. There was nothing for any light to reflect from.

He eased himself up and onto the final step, which thankfully did not move and seemed to be fixed to the base of the doorframe. As he took a moment to steady himself, he looked back down the flight of stairs, which descended into a dark curtain. Those steps that he could see, hung motionless, suspended by an unseen force.

Taking a deep breath, he turned to face the door and he placed his hands on its surface. He slightly pushed against it while he felt for a handle. The wood greeted his fingers, and he could feel the run of the grain and the bumps of small knots. His right hand closed around a metal lever, and as he pulled it downwards, there was a subtle *click*. With very little effort, the door swung inwards and a bright, silvery light washed over him; it momentarily blinded him as his eyes adjusted from his journey through the darkness.

13.

In Dreams

Gabe's brother, Kal, shifted restlessly in his sleep. A voice whispered in the shadows of an unwelcome dream. *Where is Frog? Where is the Chosen one?* The voice sounded pleasant and concerned, like someone asking after an old friend, but Kal sensed something else, something false. Something worrying.

He tried to rouse himself, but unseen hands pulled him deeper into unconsciousness.

Where is the boy? Where is Frog? This was now a demand. The voice had become menacing in tone, dark and threatening in its nature.

Kal's breathing became rapid; it escaped in short gasps, as if he were suffocating.

'I don't know,' he pleaded out loud. 'Leave me alone!'

Tell me. Tell me now. The voice seemed like a heavy weight pressing down on Kal's chest.

He couldn't wake up. He was trapped in a dark,

cloying abyss. The voice reached into him and closed like a fist around his lungs.

WHERE. IS. FROG? The words sucked the breath from him.

Kal screamed. 'Mandaran Falls!'

At that moment, the Guardian pushed back the curtain to Kal's hut. He had sensed a dark unease in the Canopy and traced it to Kal.

On his bed, Kal's body was arched, his backbone impossibly bent almost double. His body was an unhealthy, bruised blue, and his lips and face were purple, starved of oxygen.

As quickly as he could, the Guardian removed his robe. He swirled it open like the cape of a bullfighter, before he released it to fly out and fall over Kal's convulsed shape, to cover him in a protective shroud.

The hut vibrated with the sound of a deep, taunting laugh, and as the air around him pulsated, the Guardian was forced to clasp his hands over his ears. The floor gave an earthquake shudder, and then, all was still.

He rushed forwards and pulled the cape from Kal, who was now a soft shade of dull green. Much to the Guardian's relief Kal's breathing was steady and normal, and to all outwardly appearances, he looked peacefully asleep.

Gently, he placed a hand on Kal's shoulder and roused him. Kal's eyes opened, dreamily, and for a moment, he looked into the Guardian's concerned face.

Now awake, Kal became distraught and fearful. 'I told,' he said. 'I've betrayed them.' His voice quivered and tears rolled down his cheeks.

Later, after he had administered a calming potion to Kal, the Guardian stood alone in the Cradle. In the aftermath of the Afterglow, he reached his mind out.

Frog, there is danger.

He waited. No response.

Frog. Mystra. Jorge. He knows where you are.

There was nothing, just an eerie silence in his head.

They were beyond his reach, and beyond his help.

14.

BEHIND THE SILVER SCREEN

Frog stepped through the doorway and into a new, smaller cave. To his left, the waters of the Mandaran plummeted soundlessly in a great wall of liquid torrent. To his right, two large stone lions sat on their haunches on either side of a semi-circular stone basin that was decorated with three ornate patterned grooves around its front edge. The lions' mouths were frozen open in mid-roar.

A steady stream of water fell from the ceiling above, and down into the basin as if someone had left a tap running. A small hole had been eroded in its centre, and the water continued through this and on its journey, probably to join the waters of the great river somewhere below.

No gravity-defying water here, mused Frog as he stood in front of it.

Frog? Are you alright? It was Mystra's voice in his head.

Yes, yes, he replied. *Can you both hear me again?*

We thought that we had lost you, said Jorge.

I've found it. I think I've found where the figure goes.

Don't do anything until we get there. Please, pleaded Mystra.

That may take a while. I'll have to come back part of the way and guide you. It's pretty dangerous.

In the end, because the door at the top of the steps was now open and let through enough light, the others could see the floating stairway from the bottom step. However, when they had climbed up to join Frog, they agreed that they would rather have made the journey in the dark.

'It's one thing knowing that there's a bottomless pit underneath you,' said Jorge, 'but it doesn't make it any easier being able to see it!'

They assembled in front of the lions and Frog withdrew the scrap of material from his pouch.

'I am the first of four. Behind a silver screen. Where beasts roar. My place awaits me. Let me sit to give you guidance,' he read. 'Okay,' he breathed. 'The silver screen must be Mandaran Falls, and we've got two beasts that look as though they're roaring. It's my guess that this' – Frog brought out the little figurine – 'belongs here.' As they looked on, he reached out and gently placed it to sit in the stone bowl. Its curved base fitted perfectly in the little hollow, and blocked the hole at its centre, like a plug. Now that the water could not escape, the basin began to fill.

'Now what?' said Mystra. 'It's just going to overflow.'

'I think that's the point,' said Frog.

As they watched, the water reached the top of the bowl and tumbled over the three large grooves in its rim. It trickled down and began to flow along thin channels that were carved into the floor.

'Step back,' said Frog. 'It's making a pattern.'

They spread out in a semi-circle, and as they watched with curiosity, the water flowed along to wash away dust and grime and to reveal shapes carved into the stone floor.

As the water spread out, the whole of the floor became alive with the intricate shapes of letters.

'It's not a pattern,' Mystra pointed out, excitedly. 'It's writing!'

They pushed themselves back as far as they could go against a far wall.

'I can't make it out,' said Jorge. 'The writing's too big and it's all joined up.'

'It looks upside down from where I am,' pointed out Frog. 'I think that we need to be up higher to read it,' he added.

He hopped, skipped and jumped across the floor between the flowing water. When he reached one of the lions, he looked around behind it.

'Aha!' he said, triumphantly. 'Steps!'

The others watched as he climbed up the statue's

back. He rested his knees behind the animal's head and he steadied himself.

'It's a message,' he said. 'I think that it's the next clue.'

'Well. Read it out,' said an impatient Jorge.

Frog looked down at the water, which was now flowing freely across the floor in little channels that spelt out rows of words.

> *I do not answer to the north*
> *My needle shall be true only for one*
> *Until I disappear.*
> *Then revealed beneath a silver face*
> *Beware the sisters who protect the key.*

After making sure that he understood what was written, he read the words out for Mystra and Jorge.

'Does this mean that we've got to find another object?' asked Mystra.

Frog didn't answer. His mind was already working, repeating the clue over in his mind. *I do not answer to the north. My needle shall be true only for one,* he thought.

'Got it!' he shouted. 'It's a compass. Look for a compass.'

Two blank faces stared back at him.

'It's a round thing about this big.' He demonstrated with his hand. 'It usually has north, south, east, and west, marked on it, and a spinning needle set at its centre.'

They started to search around the watery letters.

'It would be a lot easier if we didn't have all this water,' said Mystra.

Frog made his way down to the stone dish. 'I'll stop the flow,' he said. He dipped his hand into the bowl and retrieved the figurine. 'Something tells me that we should hang on to this,' he said, and he put it safely back in his pouch.

The water ran away through the hole, and the bowl emptied with a gurgle. Slowly, the flow drained from the letters to leave the floor relatively dry. As he pondered over the clue, he studied some faint, carved lines that ran down the surface of the bowl and ended in tiny arrows around the small hole at its centre, which the water now trickled through.

I wonder, he thought.

He crouched down onto his hands and knees and peered beneath the basin. The escaping water obscured his view, so he reached under and felt around with his fingers. They fell upon a small oval object. He clasped his hand around it and pulled it out. It looked like a compass, made of light grey metal. He stood up and turned it towards the light. There were no markings for north, south, east or west on its face, just a pattern engraved around its edge, and what appeared to be a glass needle, which pointed away from him.

'Okaaay,' he mumbled. 'Can anyone make sense of this?' He turned to the others, and held it out for them to see.

As Mystra and Jorge handled the compass, the needle spun uncontrollably, not stopping in any position.

'That's weird. It doesn't make sense,' said Frog. 'We can't go in all directions.'

'Perhaps it's broken,' suggested Jorge.

'Let me look at it again,' said Frog. Jorge handed it back, and Frog looked down at the needle. It had stopped moving. 'Oh. Great,' he muttered.

'What?' asked Mystra.

'It's turned itself to point at the falls.' He walked towards the rushing curtain of water.

'Let me see again,' said Mystra.

Frog handed it back, and as it rested in her palm, the needle spun in a circular blur.

'I have a feeling that it will work only for you – you are the one,' she said as she passed it over to him.

Sure enough, as soon as the compass was in Frog's hand the needle stopped and pointed directly at the curtain of water.

'Well, that's no good,' said Jorge. 'We'll just have to go back the way we came in.'

Frog turned around to face them. 'I don't think that's an option.' He grimaced.

They gathered around the compass; its needle remained stubbornly motionless.

Jorge suddenly grasped the meaning. 'Jump? You expect us all to jump?' His eyebrows furrowed upon his forehead, like two thin, angry caterpillars.

'No. However, *I* have to,' said Frog. 'You two can find your way back to the bottom of the waterfall, and perhaps somehow we'll find each other.'

'No,' said Mystra, determined. 'If you go, we all go.' She looked at Jorge. 'Right?'

'You're crazy!' He looked at Mystra, and then at Frog, in disbelief.

Mystra continued to stare at Jorge. 'Right?' she repeated firmly.

In his heart, Jorge knew that there was no option. He nodded in resignation, and his complexion suddenly matched the colour of the grey rocks around them.

Frog put the compass into his pouch and securely tied the pull-string.

'Alright,' he breathed. 'Let's not hang about and delay the inevitable.' He stepped up to the edge, the cascade of water centimetres from his nose. The others stood either side of him. 'Do we jump together or one at a time?'

'I don't trust myself to be last,' admitted Jorge. 'So hopefully, I'll see you all on the other side.' With his own grim determination, and to their surprise, he jumped, and was gone.

'Now who's crazy?' said Frog.

He felt Mystra's hand in his, and she looked at him with a slight, nervous smile. 'Together?'

Frog gazed back, momentarily lost in her emerald green eyes.

'Do you believe in magic?' he asked.

'Of course,' she replied.

Without another word, they stepped out into the unknown.

15.

White Water

A curtain of churning, bubbling torrent devoured them. The noise boomed and echoed in their heads like the deafening sound of a raging thunderstorm. The waters carried them down with such speed that they imagined the fall would never end.

Frog felt Mystra's hand slip away from him. He turned his head to see her disappear into the silver-grey, boiling flood. Desperately, he pushed his thoughts out to her and Jorge, but the rolling roar of water filled every crack of his mind, so that the words were never formed.

Fear struck him like a knife in his back. He gasped a frozen breath as his mind was filled with an image of their drowned, lifeless shapes, smashed and broken on vicious black rocks.

The vision swirled and changed. The black rocks morphed into a hideously shaped human head, and their limp bodies formed its eyes, nose and mouth.

All other sound ceased, to be replaced by a voice,

a whisper that reached inside of Frog and turned his stomach into a knot, which twisted tighter with every word.

Surrender to me! Be the instrument of my bidding. Show me the path to the Tree of Spells.

He didn't feel as if he was falling anymore. The water around him became motionless. The white foam of the waterfall hung, suspended around him, unmoving. The illusion of time stood still.

You will not succeed without me. Join me and I will give you such powers the like of which you have never imagined.

Frog knew the voice. It had threatened him before. He gritted his teeth, summoning up resolve and willpower. *I know you, and I am not afraid to say your name. Maelstrom!*

The image fluttered like interference on a television screen.

Give in! Give in to me now else I will end your puny existence and let you fall.

Frog called upon all that he had learnt. He filled his mind with images of the Chosen – those who held a bond with him across the Dimensions, and his forehead shimmered and glowed with a golden light. It drowned out the whispering voice. The vile face fragmented like a shattered mirror.

YOU DO NOT CONTROL MY DESTINY! Frog shouted as loud as he could, and the words echoed in his mind.

The roar of Mandaran Falls vibrated through him and he hit the water. In an instant, his world became a swirling, watery tempest where his confused mind struggled with his body to understand where the surface might be. He wanted so much to open his mouth and drink the liquid of oblivion. He closed his eyes and stopped struggling, and he gave himself to the power of the Mandaran.

★★★

Mystra rested amongst the reeds, her body half in, half out of the eddying water. She had dragged herself to the bank, and had then collapsed with exhaustion. Waterlogged and bedraggled, she stared up at a cloudless sky, the white noise of the falls a soundtrack to her thoughts.

Frog. Jorge. Where are you?

There was no response.

'Nothing,' she said out loud. The word sounded final and resolute in her head.

She sat up, alerted by an unseen sense. A slight tremor rippled in the earth beneath her. Quickly, she rose to her feet. From the opposite side of the bank, a huge splintered branch flew from out of the forest. It arced through the air and the remnants of its leaves followed behind it like a green vapour trail. Mystra surveyed its journey, to watch it smash noisily into the undergrowth just to the left of her.

Her attention returned to the opposite bank, alerted by the destructive sounds of the forest being ripped apart. A cloud of leaves, severed branches and tree trunks scattered high into the air as if thrown up by a vicious tornado. Her colours became muddy greens and browns as she felt the pain of the trees.

Six enormous Drak swept through the treeline and onto the edge of the opposite bank. Their tentacles swished in the air like angry snakes, and they dismissively cast aside broken remnants of ancient trees. For a moment, she studied them in silence; then a tentacle reached out menacingly towards her.

'Run, Mystra. Run!' she screamed at herself.

She plunged into the undergrowth; leaves and thin branches slapped against her face and skin as she rushed recklessly in eager escape.

They'll be on me before I have a chance, she thought.

She realised that she would be safe only hidden underground. She needed to look for anything that she could crawl into.

Behind her, the Drak waded into the water, creating enormous swells, which flooded over the banks. The evil callousness of Lord Maelstrom was within them, and in their determination to catch Mystra, they continued with their ripping, destructive attack on the forest.

★★★

Frog slowly brought his head up from beneath the water, to surface under a rocky overhang. He removed a hollow reed from his mouth; it's simplicity as a breathing aid had kept him hidden and saved his life.

He watched with concern, as the Drak smashed their way into the forest on the opposite bank. He was torn with a choice. Should he continue on his own in the hope that they would all find each other or, at the risk of being caught, should he now try to help Mystra?

Mystra's voice appeared in his head. *Frog. If you hear me, don't worry. We'll find you. Jorge was swept downriver towards the white water, search for him.*

He felt for his pouch and brought out the compass. The arrow pointed downstream, towards the bubbling white foam of the rapids.

He hauled himself out of the water and into the thick bushes; here he found a slightly overgrown but nevertheless usable path, which appeared to follow the bank of the river in the direction of white water. He moved as fast as he could, pushing aside troublesome branches, and as he went, he kept an eye on the opposite bank. Even though the forest had swallowed up the sounds of the Drak in their pursuit of Mystra, he winced every time he made a noise as he scrambled through the foliage.

The sound of fast-flowing water as it thrashed over rocks began to fill his ears. Now and again, through the tangled shrubbery, he caught glimpses of white rolling waves. The trail opened out, and the vegetation began to make way for a clearer, rock-littered path. His clothes began to steam from the heat of the sun, although the humidity of the forest meant that they would never truly dry out.

The bank to his right gave way to a small, pebble-strewn beach, and he dropped down to land on it. His feet crunched on polished, wet stones as he made his way over to the water's edge where restless waves splashed at the shingle. He stared out at a cluster of large grey boulders, which jutted up from the white surf like giant broken teeth as the angry, rolling water threw itself upon them.

Without warning, a Drak crashed through the trees opposite. It twisted a bough and splintered it in half with its great tentacles, and then it threw both chunks across the river at Frog. One piece struck a boulder and cartwheeled past him, much too close for comfort, whilst the other fell short to splash into the swirling waters. The Drak strode forwards, and in that moment Frog knew that he could not outrun it.

He made an instant and reckless decision. 'I'm fed up with getting wet,' he complained to himself as he half jumped, half waded into the water. His arms stretched out to grasp the mangled log, which was now caught in the current and drifting towards the faster-moving flow. The Drak plunged into the river, and Frog took one desperate lunge. His hands seized the coarse bark and he wrapped his arms over the chunk of wood, and prayed that it would find him a safe passage through the approaching white-water hell.

As the undertow greedily pulled at his legs, and the world spun around him in a wet, roaring haze, he wondered if this time he had taken one risk too many.

Sooner or later, even my luck is going to run out, he thought.

16.

DOWNRIVER

Helped on by a small avalanche of loose earth and leaves, Mystra slithered down the side of a steep embankment. She spotted the hollow end of a large, long-time felled tree, and she scrambled on her hands and knees into the dark tunnel. An earthy, animal scent filled her senses.

She hoped that whatever creature the hiding place might belong to, that it was not at home or, if it was, that it was feeling friendly. As she crawled further in, the light of the entrance faded, and she found her way blocked by a wall of hardened mud and debris. She felt the first vibrations of the approaching Drak above her, and she had just enough room to curl herself into a sitting position, with her knees pulled up to her chest and her back against the rough wood.

She held her breath.

The ground shook with an almighty thud as a Drak landed next to her hiding place, and it let out its foghorn wail. 'Gooooraaah!' She heard the awful sound of splintering wood as a tree was torn from its roots, then a resounding crash as her sanctuary was struck, either by the infuriated Drak or by something that it had thrown. Her hiding place rolled with the impact, and she was turned over and over, as it fell out of control, and spun down into a shallow gully.

As she lay in semi-darkness, her arms and legs uncomfortably twisted, she caught her breath again as the angry sounds of the searching Drak receded into the forest.

Her head swirled, and she straightened her legs. Slowly, she crawled towards the light at the end of the trunk. She used her ability to camouflage herself, and her colours took on the same browns of the muddy earth and the bark of the trunk. She craned her neck out and into the open. The destructive sounds of the Drak moved away into the distance.

She eased herself out. All wildlife had fled, and in the unnatural silence, she examined herself for injuries. Apart from a couple of grazes to her arms and legs, there was nothing serious.

'That was lucky,' she consoled herself.

She plucked a couple of broad leaves from an overhanging plant, and rubbed them gently on her injuries as she took in the devastation above and around her. A wide area had been trashed and flattened. The violence that had been inflicted on the trees was indiscriminate and vicious.

Her mind reached out to Frog and Jorge, and after several attempts, she resigned to the fact that they were too far away. Stubbornly, she would not even let the suggestion enter her thoughts, that they were harmed, or even worse.

She decided to head for the river and follow it downstream. Jorge had been carried that way and she had a feeling that it was the direction that the compass would take Frog. After climbing out of the gully, she turned in the opposite direction of the marauding Drak.

Eventually, she was rewarded with the roaring of the rapids as the sound filtered through the trees, and she turned to follow the course of the river. Here, the grass grew taller than her and she pushed herself through the stalks to eventually come out above a steep bank, which overlooked a wide, slow-moving stretch of water.

There, on the opposite bank sat two figures. The body of one shifted and fluttered with the soft colours of the forest, whilst the other remained a pale, pinkish hue. The tops of their tunics hung, dripping, in the branches of a tree, along with their water-sodden packs. Frog and Jorge sat cross-legged, and appeared to be comparing their grazes and bruises.

Frog was the first to look up; he gave her a big, toothy grin, and Jorge waved a hand and smiled a relieved welcome.

'Nice to see that you two have been relaxing while I've been chased by Drak,' she shouted.

The smile disappeared from Frog's face. 'Are you sure that they haven't followed you?'

'No. They went off in the other direction quite a while ago,' replied Mystra. She surveyed the river. 'How are we going to get back together? I think that the banks are too steep here.'

Frog held up the compass. 'It's still pointing downriver. I suggest we walk in that direction until it gets shallow enough for us to cross over.'

That decision made, Mystra moved on, and the boys continued their journey shortly after. As Frog followed Jorge through the rough grasses of the riverbank, he reflected on how luck or magic had saved him once again, this time from the fury of the rapids.

The log that he had clung on to swept him away from the Drak, and caught a flow of water, which was channelled between two enormous rocks. The force was enough to propel him and the log out into the next churning wall of white water, as if he had been shot out of a cannon. He'd just had enough time to take a deep breath before the current forced him down into a whirling, bubbling cauldron. He hung on with all his might, all the while reminding himself that the log was bound to float to the surface and take him with it, hopefully before his lungs exploded!

It seemed an age, and as his chest strained and burned with the desire to breathe, the muffled underwater sound of the rapids was replaced with a clear roaring in his ears. He hit the surface face up, clinging desperately to his wooden life buoy. It felt as if there were half a dozen fire hoses aimed at him. Spray stung his face and blinded him as he was thrown around like a toy in a washing machine. Several times he felt a sickening crunch as the lump of wood struck rocks and boulders, and he waited for the moment when it would be his bones splintering from the next impact.

The water carried him over a steep drop and he let out an involuntary, rollercoaster 'Whoa!' Again, he went under for a few moments until the log brought him back up to bob about like a frenzied cork. It spun around, and he faced something that knotted up his stomach like a piece of dried-out leather.

The torrent in front of him was gushing into a narrow channel between two more rocks. With immense power, it forced the water right into the face of a huge grey boulder – he would be pulverised, and death would be instant. He kicked out frantically as if he could somehow, against all odds, swim backwards against nature's fury. As the current thrust him towards the inescapable exit, he closed his eyes.

In his head, he cried out to his mother and father. Not a cry for help, but a cry of love and longing.

He saw images of their faces, smiling down at him, gentle and calm.

I'll just let go and it'll be over in an instant, he thought.

There was a jolt. His chest slammed up against the log and he gasped. The pressure on his back was tremendous as the water pummelled into him now that he had become an obstruction. His eyes opened to realise that the log had been wedged lengthways between the two boulders and the force of the water was keeping it in place, but that same force was now threatening to pull him underneath the log and to certain death. He tried to pull himself up, to claw his way out of the water, but his strength was sapping away; he was nearing exhaustion.

As he felt a last flicker of hope being snatched from him, a dark shadow fell across his face. Over the sounds of the gushing water, he heard a voice.

'Are you going to grab my hand or not?' Frog looked up to see Jorge's welcome face, and an outstretched arm. Without any further encouragement, he grasped out with both hands. Jorge proved his strength and dragged Frog out, and onto the rock, where he rested open mouthed and gasping like a landed fish.

Why do I have to do everything the hard way? Frog thought, as he brought his senses back to the present.

In contrast, Jorge's own journey had been less dramatic. He'd been washed through the first group of rocks and forced to the bottom by the current.

In the grey swirling water, his hands had found the trailing roots of an overhanging tree, which he'd used to pull himself up to the surface and out of the river.

Presently, the boys reached a wide curve, where the river flowed lazily, and over time, a bank of silt and gravel had formed into a shallow ford. It was here, Mystra waited patiently. Frog smiled to himself as he watched her colours ripple with pleasure at seeing them safely reunited.

'So, which side of the river should we follow?' said Jorge, as they came together on the mustard-yellow shingle.

Frog held out the compass and they watched as the needle turned to point to the left of the river, where a stream wound itself from the forest.

'At least we're still going in the opposite direction to those Drak,' said Mystra.

'I have a feeling that they knew where to find us,' said Frog.

'You mean, someone knows where we're going?' said Jorge.

'Well, there's only one other person who's interested in what we're looking for,' said Frog. 'And he's managed to get into my head recently. Have any of you had that problem?'

The others looked at him with surprise.

'He got into your head?' said Jorge, as the colours paled from his face.

'It's me that he wants to control,' explained Frog. 'I don't think that he'll bother you,' he added, optimistically.

'I'll remember you said that,' said Jorge. 'Come on, we'd better get moving. It'll be night soon.'

'Is it that late?' asked Frog. 'How do you know?'

'We just do,' said Mystra. 'It's part of our connection to Tropal.'

'Just give me a warning,' said Frog. 'It's a bit unsettling for the sun to go out when you least expect it!'

As they pushed back a pathway, and re-entered the forest, Frog became aware of the background noise, the animals and the birds couldn't help but announce their presence, but nothing seemed disturbed, nothing flapped or skittered away in fright.

'Have you been here before?' Frog asked Jorge. 'Do you recognise this part of the forest?'

'I've looked down on the falls and the rapids, but I've never ventured this far along the course of the Mandaran,' he replied. 'How's that compass doing?'

'Straight ahead,' said Frog. 'It's following the passage of the stream.'

The switch from day to night startled him, and he blinked several times before his eyes adjusted. An unseen root caused him to stumble to the ground, and he sat there, staring accusingly up at Mystra. 'A warning would have been good,' he chided her.

'Sorry. I forgot,' said Mystra, sheepishly.

'No harm done,' he sighed as he got to his feet. 'I guess that we should think about setting up a camp for the night,' he suggested.

The long-off echo of a foghorn-like moan filtered over the treetops.

'Let's just put a bit more distance between us and them,' said Jorge, as he pushed his way through the moonlit-dappled shrubbery.

17.

DARK THREATS

Every Dimension has its evil side. From the dawn of creation, all worlds have a shadowed stain that simmers and seethes in hidden, dark places. It waits for something, or someone, to rouse it from its slumber.

Tropal was no exception, and Lord Maelstrom's presence stirred the dormant evil. He went in search of it, through the underground caves and into the secret places deep beneath the earth, until he found the beast and released the ancient chains that bound it. He breathed his dark powers into it and commanded it to do his bidding. He smiled with satisfaction as it stretched its unkempt wings, and he relished the thought of when he would send it out on a mission of death and destruction.

Other ancient evils came to him like whispers in the night, and he moulded and shaped them into living, breathing servants. They were his tiny, invisible Whisperers, his sowers of doubt and hopelessness. Their voices were filled with all the fears and dreads of every soul. As soon as you heard the mournful rustling from their thin lips, your heart would begin to sink, your courage would fail. Despair would drag you down to surrender and defeat. You became an empty shell, a sleepwalker hypnotised by their words of misery.

He despatched two such Whisperers with one objective – 'Seek out his companions and drain them of all hope,' he commanded. 'Make them yours and turn them against him. Then bring them all to me.'

18.

THE KEY

They emerged into a clearing, formed by a circular ring of trees. At its centre sat a round pond, which fed the stream that they had been following. The flat, unmoving surface of the pond gave the illusion of a sheet of un-blemished glass.

'Which way now?' asked Jorge.

Frog looked at the compass. The dial was blank, and only a smooth, unmarked face remained. 'The needle. It's gone!' he said.

'Here, let me see,' said Jorge.

They gathered around the compass.

'Is this it? Is this where we are supposed to be?' asked Mystra.

'I do not answer to the north. My needle shall be true only for one. Until I disappear. Then revealed beneath a silver face. Beware the sisters who protect the key,' repeated Frog. 'The needle's disappeared, so now we have to find a silver face.'

They glanced around the clearing.

'It's got to be around here somewhere,' said Jorge. 'I'll look over there; you two spread out.'

Mystra didn't move.

'What's the matter?' said Frog.

'I've already found it,' she smiled, obviously pleased with herself.

'How can you? You haven't even moved,' complained Jorge.

'I didn't have to,' she continued to smile.

'Well. Where is it?' he asked.

Mystra said nothing, but tilted her head, and her smile, heavenward. The others followed her gaze.

Shining down on them was a silvery face.

'Of course,' said Frog. 'The moon.'

'The clue is here, hidden in the clearing under the moonlight,' said Mystra.

'So we've still got to search.' Jorge shrugged. 'But for what?'

'A key,' said Frog.

'What sort of key?' asked Mystra.

'I don't know,' said Frog.

'And what about the sisters?' she asked.

'Stop asking questions that we haven't got the answers to,' said Jorge; his patience had become worn by tiredness. 'Just look for anything that is shaped like a key.'

'Okay. Grumpy,' said Mystra as she sidled away. 'You're not the only one who's tired. Perhaps we should just take a short rest and get some sleep,' she added.

'No can do,' said Frog. 'We need the moon, and if we sleep past daybreak we'll have to sit here until tomorrow night when it comes out again, to find the key. With the Drak wandering around, I'd rather we didn't take that long.'

Jorge sighed, wearily. 'We'd better get on with it then.'

Because none of them had noticed how far into the clearing they had got when the needle vanished, they had to search the whole area. They scoured well into the bushes; then they crawled on their hands and knees, feeling through the blades of grass with their fingers, until after more than an hour Jorge stopped.

'That's it. I give up. I'm too tired,' he complained. 'I thought that it would be easier than this.'

'It's not supposed to be easy at all,' said Frog. 'Then revealed beneath a silver face. Beware the sisters who protect the key,' he repeated to himself. He stood up and walked to the edge of the pond. 'Of course!' he realised.

'It's in there, isn't it,' said Jorge, making more of a statement than a question.

Frog pointed to the moon's perfect reflection. 'Sometimes it's that simple.' He started to remove his sword, and tunic. 'Nice evening for a dip,' he said, resignedly.

'I'll do it,' volunteered Mystra.

'Thanks for offering, Mystra, but remember what the Guardian said: I have to be the one who actually finds the clues.'

He slid his bare legs into the water, and it felt bathtub warm to his skin. Ripples rolled out in a procession across its surface to turn the mirror image of the moon's face into a distorted scream. Frog pushed himself out to the centre of the pool, suddenly aware that his splashes sounded dull and lifeless. The water felt thick and heavy on his body, almost like oil.

'Count up to sixty. If I'm not back, come and get me,' he smiled nervously.

He filled his lungs with one long intake of sweet air, and then he duck-dived into the unknown.

'Two. Three. Four,' began Jorge, out loud.

As soon as Frog's feet had disappeared, the water became instantly and ominously calm. As if he was never there.

Below the surface, he struggled to see clearly. It was as though he was looking through the thick lenses of glasses made for someone with very bad eyesight. Everything was distorted and out of focus. Wavering shafts of moonlight streaked past him and melted into unimagined depths. He twisted his body around, and screwed his eyes up as he tried to glimpse the edge of the pool. The whole thing was only about five metres across, so it couldn't be that far out of reach, he assured himself.

A shimmer of light attracted his attention. One moonbeam, straight and unmoving, lit up a dark hollow where something glistened. It seemed to beckon him.

He kicked his legs and pushed his body towards it, his arms outstretched and reaching. His movements seemed slow, and despite the effort he used, he didn't move as fast as he expected to. Three kicks and he still hadn't touched the side. His chest started to tighten. He gave one more strong push and felt relieved as his hands connected with the slippery, reed-covered wall of the pool.

To his left there was a small hollowed-out alcove, where a silver moonbeam illuminated a large, ornamental key. He reached his hand out towards it – that was when she came at him.

The corpse-pale form of a woman materialised out of nowhere. She was clothed in a muddy grey dress, made up of thin strands of material, which floated around her in slow motion, and her long white hair trailed behind her like fine strips of torn cloth. Her eyes were empty and black, and her face was both beautiful and frightening. She grabbed at Frog's arms with her bony hands, and tried to pin them to his sides. He sensed that she meant to embrace him and pull him down with her, to drown him in the murky depths below.

His lungs began to burn as they demanded that he exhale and take in fresh oxygen, and he looked up to see the glass sheet of the surface further above him than he felt it should be.

His cheeks puffed out and precious air escaped his lips in a frenzied stream of bubbles, which scattered away upwards. He brought his knees up between their bodies and kicked out to push her away. For a moment, he was free of her grasp. He clawed at the long reeds, frantically pulling himself upwards with his arms. Out of the corner of his eye, the watery shape of another similar looking woman, rose from the depths towards him, her face contorted with rage, and her bloodless arms outstretched to grasp him. As he felt the last rattle of air escape from his lungs, he heaved himself up in a desperate attempt to reach the surface.

The others had been leaning over the pool's edge, peering down to get a glimpse of Frog's shape.

'Fifty-nine,' said Jorge, as Mystra prepared to dive in.

They jumped back in alarm, as Frog's head and shoulders burst out of the water. His arms thrashed at the bank and he sucked in air and gasped. 'Pull me out! Pull me out!'

They grabbed his arms and dragged him onto the grass, and as his legs cleared the edge, Mystra caught sight of a pale, bony hand as it grasped at thin air before it slipped back into the black surface of the pool.

They leant over Frog as he coughed up gobbets of slime-like water, whilst desperately gulping for air. Gradually, he brought his breathing under control, but he found it hard to swallow because of an unpleasant taste in his mouth.

'I need some clean water, please. Just something to rinse my mouth out.'

Jorge passed him his canteen and Frog sucked it in, before swishing it around and spitting it out with a grimace.

'What happened?' said Mystra.

'I've seen the key,' said Frog. 'But it's guarded by what I think are water sprites, and they're not at all friendly.'

'Where is it?' asked Jorge.

'It's just underneath us, a few metres down.'

'What if two of us go in,' suggested Mystra. 'One could hold them off while the other grabbed the key.'

'It's too risky,' replied Frog. 'I was lucky to escape from two of them, and who knows how many more there are, waiting down there.'

For a while, they sat there in silence, each of them searching in their own minds for a solution.

Without a word, Frog stood, and walked to the edge of the pool.

'What are you doing?' asked an anxious Jorge.

'I've got an idea,' said Frog. 'Just be ready to haul me out when I come up.'

Before they could stop him, he jumped in, feet first. He held his nose with one hand and grabbed the talisman on the chain around his neck with the other. By the time he was submerged, he was invisible.

The disturbance in the water alerted the two sprites, and they shifted uneasily as their black, empty eyes searched for their prey. Frog had taken a risk, and only half filled his lungs with air so that his body would sink slowly towards the little recess where the key was hidden.

As he got within arm's reach of the key, the sprites sensed that someone was in the water with them. They turned their ashen faces to look straight at where Frog drifted, unseen.

The ghostly nymphs opened their toothless mouths in silent screams, and lunged blindly towards him. He reached in and grabbed the key, and then he kicked for all his might towards the surface as adrenalin gave him a much-needed surge in strength.

To keep the power of his talisman secret, and so that Mystra and Jorge could see him as he broke the surface; he released his grip on the chain and reached up with both arms. Two pairs of hands clasped around his wrists and hauled him out onto the grass. Behind him, the water erupted as a bloodless face rose up; its black and empty mouth screamed in rage and fury like a wailing Banshee, and it clawed at the air in vain, before it sunk back into the pond.

They all shuffled nervously backwards, away from the edge of the water.

'You really are crazy!' said Jorge.

'And stupid,' scolded Mystra. 'You could have drowned.'

'But I didn't,' smiled Frog, as he held up the key in triumph.

They looked up as the key was silhouetted against the moon, and the same realisation struck them at the same time.

'It's made out of shapes and letters!' announced an excited Mystra.

Frog squinted in the moonlight. 'Sea-epofi-hedead?'

'Let me see,' said Jorge.

Frog handed the key to him. He held it aloft, turning it in his hand as he did so. With a nervous sigh, Jorge turned to Mystra.

'Have you ever heard of what is beyond the everglades?'

She gave Jorge a worried glance. 'You mean, the Valley? But that's just a folktale.'

'I'm thinking about the other folktale, about what protects the entrance to the Valley,' prompted Jorge.

'Fable or real,' said Mystra, 'it's not somewhere that I really want to go.'

Frog noticed that their colours had become subdued and dull. 'Will someone please tell me what you're going on about?'

Jorge held up the key once more. He pointed to the writing. 'I've seen this lettering before, on a manuscript of the Guardian's. S-W-A-M-P-O-F-T-H-E-D-E-A-D,' he spelt out. 'Swamp of the Dead!'

'I guess that it's not going to be Disney World, then,' said Frog. Their faces looked at him as if he'd spoken in a foreign language. 'Sorry. Just me trying to be funny,' he explained. 'I take it that what with the skull on the key and the reference to the dead, it's not going to be a very nice place.'

'If it exists,' said Mystra, hoping for the opposite.

'It must exist,' said Frog. 'Because that's where we have to take this key.'

'If the Swamp of the Dead exists,' said Jorge, 'then so must the Valley that it guards.'

'Will someone tell me what this Valley is?' asked Frog.

'Plenty of time for that,' said Jorge. 'I think that we should move away from here and set up camp for the night in the safety of the forest. We need to get some rest if we've got the journey ahead of us that I think we have.'

They bedded down beneath the overhanging branches of an old and ancient tree. Just before they settled, both Mystra and Jorge gently stroked its crusty bark and whispered quietly to it for a few moments, thanking it for its shelter and asking for its protection.

Despite his fright in the pond, Frog slept a deep and quiet sleep. The others, however, had an uneasy night, their rest disturbed by half-dreamt images and troubling thoughts.

19.

THE SPELL OF THE GUARDIAN

The next morning, Frog awoke to find Mystra putting fresh wood on their campfire; the flames already licked greedily around the long-dead branches.

He pulled himself up onto one elbow as he wiped the tiny crusts of sleep from his eyes. 'Where's Jorge?' he asked.

'He's gone to the stream, to get breakfast,' she replied.

'And that would be?'

'Fresh fish!' announced Jorge, as he stepped into the clearing.

Frog stood, arched his back and stretched his arms as he breathed in the crisp morning air. He watched as Jorge laid three, steely-scaled fish, about the size of small trout, onto a stone slab by the fire.

'Have you just caught them?' Frog enquired.

'Caught them and cleaned them,' Jorge smiled.

Mystra put some wild herbs and mushrooms onto the fish, and folded them over. Then, using a stick, she prodded back the now red and white-hot embers from the fire, and deftly placed the stone and its cargo of fish, at its centre.

'If you want to go and throw some water on your face,' she said to Frog, 'you've got a few minutes and then these will be ready.'

It didn't take Frog long to bring himself fully awake as he washed himself with the refreshing stream water, and soon after, all three of them sat cross-legged, the broad leaves on their laps acting as plates, now strewn with the remains of the devoured fish.

'Delicious!' commented Frog, as he licked his fingers. 'And no washing-up to do. Just the way that I like it,' he beamed.

'That may well be the last really fresh food that we get to eat for a while, apart from some fruit, that is,' said Jorge.

'Why's that?' asked Frog.

'Because we're now travelling into unknown territory, at least to me it is,' he said. 'And I should imagine any food will get even scarcer as we reach the swamp. I just hope that we don't have to venture into the Valley.'

'Okay,' said Frog. 'I think that it's about time you told me about this Valley place.'

'Only the Guardian knows more than anyone

else,' said Jorge. 'But I'll tell you all that I know.' He took a drink of water.

'In the history of Tropal, there have been two conflicts; the first was when the forest was young and guarded by those who are now Immortals. I will not concern you with that tale right now, because it is the struggle between the people of the forest and the Horsemen of the Flatlands that is linked to our destination. This is the story that has been handed down through generations.

'The Horsemen wanted more and more open plains for their horses to run free, so they began to cut down the trees and flatten great swathes of forest. Despite many pleas from the forest people and warnings from the Guardian, the Horsemen continued to turn extensive areas of Tropal into Flatlands.

'Feeling threatened, the forest people dug great ditches around the edges of the forest and guarded them, day and night, until late one evening, a group of Horsemen managed to start fires in the forest. Sadly, the fires raged out of control and a whole community of forest people, men, women and children, were killed in the inferno before it was extinguished.

'Distraught, the forest people called upon the Guardian to punish the Horsemen, lest there be more bloodshed. He judged their actions to be so great a crime that he banished them to live in shame, and he confined them to the great Valley of the north. Through ancient magic, he transported them there along with their horses, and they were forbidden to leave the Valley. He placed unseen barriers of magic in the mountain passes, and he sealed its entrance with a wall of rock, surrounded by a great swamp. It was in the swamp that he lay to rest the souls of the forest people who had been killed. They would be wardens and gatekeepers, until, through an act of steadfastness and courage, the Horsemen would release them.

'It is also said that the Guardian inflicted one more act of retribution on the Horsemen, too terrible to be revealed, but if ever there came a time when the forest people and Tropal needed help, should the Horsemen answer the call, they would be set free and the punishment removed. For hundreds of years, no one has ventured near the swamp or the Valley, and we have only a simple forest shrine to the dead, as a reminder of that dark moment in Tropal's history.'

Frog ran over in his mind, what Jorge had told him.

'Okay,' he said. 'I think that I've got it all. Dead people. Weird Horsemen. A curse. However, still no mention of the Tree of Spells. I guess it's off to the Swamp of the Dead then, to find out what the key will unlock.'

Mystra looked at him. 'Does nothing scare you?'

'Of course it does,' he replied. 'But if I allow it get to me, I may as well give up and let Lord you-know-who take over.'

At that moment, deep within him, the boy who was Chris truly longed for his home.

20.

WHISPERS

As their journey progressed, the forest trees became sparse and their trunks grew much thinner. Their leaves took on a blackish-grey hue and the ground became uneven and rock-strewn. Grass and foliage struggled to grow in anything more than isolated clumps. Eventually, the forest gave way to a land of broken tree stumps, which stretched out before them like scattered, rotten teeth. It wasn't just the landscape that deteriorated, so too did the sky. In the daytime, it was as if a dirty, grey sheet had been draped over them. Even the purple disc of the sun seemed tainted and stained. To add to this, they became aware of an odour, which drifted around them and clung to their clothes. It reminded Frog of stagnant and diseased pond water.

He noticed that Mystra and Jorge's colours were losing their vibrancy, becoming faded and almost washed out like very pale pastels. Their moods became quiet and sombre. It was as though they were carrying a great, unseen weight. When he spoke or tried to make conversation, they became rude and bad-tempered towards him. A curtain had fallen over their minds. Their thoughts were hidden from him.

They moved between the lumps of withered and cracked wood, and it seemed to Frog that Mystra and Jorge were struggling to move forwards; every step seemed an effort for them.

Eventually, he couldn't bear to tolerate it any longer.

'Stop!' His voice sounded like a gunshot in the silent and lifeless terrain. 'What's happening to you? It's like you've lost all hope, as though you've given up.'

They turned and stared at him; the expressions on their faces were vague and lost. He recalled that he had seen this before, on the faces of people in the Dimensions of Castellion and Aridian, and he knew that it was Lord Maelstrom's doing.

Frog walked over to them. 'Hold hands.'

They looked at him with blank eyes.

'Here,' he said as he clasped two of their hands together.

What happened next was sudden and unpredictable, and afterwards he realised that he didn't feel the blow at the time, mainly because he wasn't expecting it.

Jorge twisted away, brought up his arm and swung the back of it against Frog's chest. His fist connected against Frog's face with enough force that it sent him toppling backwards. He lay there shocked and confused as the taste of warm blood trickled from his nose and across his lips.

'What? What's the matter with you?' he managed.

'Grab him,' Jorge spoke in a blank emotionless voice.

Mystra rushed forwards and sat herself across Frog's legs, pinning him down, while Jorge unfurled a length of vine.

Frog knew in an instant that if he let them tie him up, then he would have little chance of escaping, and whatever they intended to do with him was of evil's command.

Mystra grappled with his wrists as Jorge knelt down and looped the vine, ready to wrap it around and restrain Frog's arms. If he was to stop them, it had to be now, even if it meant hurting one or even both of them in the process.

He hadn't used his Tae-kwondo skills for quite a while; now he needed to demonstrate what he had learnt. He jerked his knees up, which forced Mystra to topple forwards and lose her grip on his wrists. Then he rolled himself sideways, to land on top of her. He looked into her still, empty eyes.

'I know that you're in there somewhere, Mystra,' he said to her.

A momentary pause nearly cost him dearly

as she brought her arms up and gripped him in a stranglehold.

Suckered! he thought to himself.

He pushed his arms between hers, forced them apart, and swung a clenched fist across her jaw. 'Sorry,' he said. Her eyes rolled up into her head and her body became limp. It was then that he felt Jorge grab him by the hair and pull him backwards. Off balance, he was helpless as Jorge tugged on the handle of Frog's sword, and the blade slid from its scabbard. He looked up into Jorge's unseeing pupils; the dull steel of the sword hung in the air, waiting for its weight to be brought down across Frog's head.

For just a moment, Jorge hesitated, and that was when Frog kicked out to swipe Jorge's ankles from beneath him. As Jorge fell, Frog reached up and grabbed the wayward sword. With a grimace of regret, he brought the metal nub of the hilt across Jorge's temple, and he collapsed into an unconscious heap next to Mystra.

By the time their eyelids flickered open to reveal their vacant, staring eyes, Frog had used the vine to tie their hands together with Mystra's sandwiched between Jorge's. She seemed not to notice her swollen lip and the small dribble of blood on her mouth and chin, any more than Jorge acknowledged the now blue-yellow, egg-shaped lump on the side of his head.

Frog crouched down on his haunches in front of them. 'Something's got to you, and as far as I know, there's only one way to find out what's going on.'

He clasped both of his hands around theirs, closed his eyes, and began to repeat, 'Let the Light free us from evil. Let the Light free us from evil…'

His forehead lit up with the familiar golden glow of the Chosen, however, he sensed that something was amiss and he opened his eyes. The Light had spread out from him, but before it could make contact with Mystra and Jorge, it seemed to be held back by a hidden barrier.

'Let the Light free us from evil,' he said, loudly.

Mystra and Jorge remained silent, and he noticed that they now stared through him as though he weren't there.

'Come on, guys,' he encouraged. 'Say it. Let the Light free us from evil.'

Nothing. No reaction.

He looked at how the Light was being curved, reflected away from his friends.

'No!' he said, firmly. 'You will not have them.'

He reached forwards and pushed his head against theirs; they tried to wrench away, so he clasped his hands around their heads to ensure that he kept contact with them.

'Let the Light free us from evil! Let the Light free us from evil!' He was shouting now, louder and louder. 'Let the Light free us from evil!'

There was a surge of brilliant gold light as it enveloped all three of them. Mystra and Jorge's eyes glowed like fierce burning suns, and their hair rippled as if caught in a wave of static.

'Let the Light free us from evil,' they finally echoed.

Frog pulled away as two creatures materialised. They were about twenty centimetres in size, and they sat, uncomfortably, on Mystra and Jorge's shoulders. At first, he thought that their feathered wings made them look like miniature angels. They looked at him with their electric-blue eyes, and it was then that he heard their snake-like voices in his head, whispering like the rustling of dried leaves.

You have no hope. You are worthless. Everything that you have done has been meaningless. Listen to the fear in your heart and surrender to despair.

For just a moment, he glimpsed what they really were – dark, twisted shapes of wretchedness. Thin, ragged-winged negatives of fairy-like creatures with slit-thin eyes and needle pointed teeth. They hissed silently with spite and malice.

'Let the Light free us from evil,' continued Mystra and Jorge.

Frog watched as the restraining vines untied themselves and slipped to the ground. Burning suns shone brightly on their foreheads, and they stood up to join hands with him in a circle. The creatures opened their mouths and screamed a long high-pitched wail, then their shapes folded inwards and they imploded into empty space.

For a moment, Mystra and Jorge stood radiant and smiling.

As the Light of the Chosen slowly faded like a reluctant sunset, Frog noticed a circle of fresh green grass spreading out from where they stood.

He was the first to speak. 'Are you okay?'

'I feel as if I've been in a long sleep,' said Jorge.

'Yes, it's weird,' said Mystra. 'It's like I've had a really bad dream that I can't remember.'

'What happened to us?' asked Jorge.

Frog looked at them. They seemed healthy and refreshed. Their skin was rippling with vibrant oranges and yellows. He also noticed that neither of them showed any signs of the injuries that he had inflicted upon them.

'I guess that the only way to explain it is that you were sort of, possessed.'

'What?' they echoed in disbelief.

'Over the last couple of days, you both became quite irritable and withdrawn, until today, when you really lost it. You' – he pointed at Mystra – 'sat on me and tried to tie me up.'

Jorge laughed.

'And *you* tried to kill me.'

They both looked at him with astonishment.

'Oh yes,' he nodded. He wiped his nose and lip with the back of his sleeve, and indicated to the smear of dried blood. 'Do you think that I got this by walking into a tree?'

Mystra moved to him, concerned. 'Is it broken?'

Frog tentatively prodded his nose. 'I don't think so. It's stopped bleeding now.'

He used his water bottle to rinse his face with clean water, and he explained in more detail what had happened.

'Those creatures, whatever they were, must have been whispering into your heads for the last couple of days, feeding off any doubts and fears in your memories. Once I managed to combine the full force of the Chosen, you found the strength needed to sweep away the spell that they'd thrown over you. From the look of you, I think that you'll be alright now, though I'm not sure if we've seen the last of those things.'

'I'm really sorry,' apologised Jorge.

'Not your fault,' Frog smiled. 'Looks like Lord pain-in-the-backside has found something new to attack us with. I'm just worried about how many more of them there could be, and when he'll send them next.'

'Best we get on with what we have to do, then,' said Jorge, with fresh determination.

All three turned and looked out across the desolate landscape.

'It looks as though someone's dropped a nuclear bomb,' remarked Frog.

'Explain,' said Mystra.

'It's a weapon of mass destruction that any world would be better off without. Where I come from, we have invented and discovered many wonderful and fantastic things, but I think that the creation of the nuclear bomb was probably our darkest hour.'

They stared out in silence at the bleak scene before them, until Frog wrinkled his nose and spoke again.

'I guess from the smell, that we're getting closer to the swamp.'

21.

THE SWAMP OF THE DEAD

The ground squelched like spongy black earth, which oozed dark liquid from beneath their feet. It was a strange sensation, and all the more disturbing because, unlike mud, it didn't cling or stick to their boots or clothes. Even the rotting stumps of the long-dead forest had now disappeared beneath the foul-smelling terrain. Noises began to bubble and gurgle from pools of tired black water around them, as putrid gases escaped in thin jets of luminous mist and puffs of vile green clouds. They pulled their tunics up around their mouths and noses in a futile attempt to screen out the nauseating stink.

'Phew!' exclaimed Frog. 'It's worse than dog farts!'

Even though the smell clung to the back of their throats, Mystra and Jorge burst into a bout of hysterical laughter, which Frog could not contain himself from joining in. They laughed and coughed, sharing a humour that did not belong in such a forsaken place. It was Mystra who brought their mirth to an abrupt end.

'Night is coming,' she said, and her head tilted up towards the dishwater murk that loomed high above them.

Night fell in a blink, and as they stood together, a symphony of discordant, bubbling noises gurgled around them. It took a moment for them to realise that the obnoxious smell and gases produced an unexpected benefit for them. A green fluorescent glow lit up their surroundings – the results of escaping methane and small decaying algae.

Frog had seen a similar effect displayed from the night-time phosphorus in the waters of a Scottish lake whilst he was on a family holiday in his own Dimension. A memory of his other life skirted the edge of his mind, and then it dissolved behind a curtain.

'If it didn't pong so much, it would be beautiful,' he muttered.

'Look!' said Mystra, pointing ahead them.

'It's a path,' said Jorge.

A line of bright, shining green lights stretched out like a twisting, luminous snake to reveal a narrow footway that worked itself though the myriad of glutinous, gurgling pools.

'Okay,' said Frog. 'It's about time that we had some help. We'll need to walk in single file. I'll lead the way.'

'I'll bring up the rear, that is if you don't mind walking between us,' Jorge volunteered to Mystra.

'Please be careful not to slip. I don't fancy having to pull someone out of that stinking mud,' said Frog.

'I don't fancy having to walk along with that person *after* we've pulled them out!' said Mystra.

The green mist washed backwards and forwards across the pathway like the waves of a restless tide, and quite often, they had to stop until the path was clear to see again. Through the half-light, Frog noticed that what he at first thought were dark clouds ahead of them were in fact the outline of a high cliff wall, which stretched in the distance, forming a barricade across their path.

'Looks like we might have some climbing to do,' he indicated.

'It's a long way off,' said Jorge. 'I don't think that we'll reach it until at least tomorrow.'

'We can't travel all night,' said Mystra. 'We need to rest.'

'Well, we certainly can't camp on this narrow path,' said Frog. 'I don't know about you, but I'd like to keep moving just to get out of this stink.'

Silently, they all resigned to the fact that they would have to keep travelling for as long as they could.

They continued to pick their way through the swamp, and although they kept up a good pace,

Frog noticed that the cliff wall did not seem to be getting any closer. He was just about to voice this observation, when the mist rose up in front of them in a thick, sickly green barrier.

'Now what?' he complained. 'If this keeps up, we'll have to find another way.'

'No chance of that,' said Jorge.

Frog and Mystra turned to see a similar obstruction had also appeared behind them.

To either side, the surface of the swamp ceased its gurgling emissions and took on the appearance of a smooth, black, oil-like liquid. They watched with unease as countless forms of ghostly, shimmering figures rose up, illuminated from the depths, and thin rays of grey light filtered through the oily surface to ripple eerily against the overhanging mist.

Frog instinctively drew his sword. He felt trapped, and experience had taught him to be ready to defend himself.

'Whatever you can fight with, I suggest that you ready yourselves,' he warned the others as countless semi-transparent figures ascended on either side of them, to float effortlessly as if suspended on soft cushions of air.

'It's the dead,' whispered Mystra.

Jorge reached across and gently brought Frog's sword arm down. 'I don't think that will do you any good,' he said.

'Look at them, so many,' said Mystra. Her voice trembled with emotion.

Frog looked around him. He studied the sorrowful expressions on the faces of the men, women and children who now surrounded them. Each one of them was simply clothed in long, hooded robes, which shifted in smoky patterns around their transparent shapes.

He could sense the sadness behind their colourless eyes, and he felt their longing to be released from the chains of the past and the wrongdoing of the Horsemen.

The spectral shape of a woman drifted towards them. Even her monochrome form did not lessen her beauty. She moved towards Frog and settled a short distance away to silently examine him with her curious eyes.

Her voice, when it came, was soft and clear, almost as if she was whispering right into their ears. She addressed Frog.

'You are a stranger to this world. What business have you with the Horsemen?'

Frog steadied his nerve and replied. 'How do you know that I have business with them?'

'Why else would you walk the path of the dead?' came her reply.

Mystra moved forwards. 'We seek the Tree of Spells.'

A faint whisper passed amongst the shapes, with the hushed sound of a gentle breeze.

'Forest child, why would the Tree of Spells concern you?'

Mystra placed her hand on Frog's shoulder. 'Great evil has come to Tropal. This is the Chosen one sent to seek out and protect the Tree.'

The woman studied Frog for a moment. 'Would it be that you are also the one who could bring our deliverance?'

Frog stared into her gaze, and for a moment, he felt the heavy weight of loneliness. He felt claustrophobic and homesick. Her sadness, and the longing of freedom emanating from the spectres floating around him, was almost overpowering. It took all of his strength to stop himself from running recklessly and blindly away and into the surrounding swamp.

'If it is in my power to set you free,' he said quietly, 'then I will gladly do so.'

'To set us free, you must also set the Horsemen free – they must agree to fight against the evil that you speak of.'

'How do I get to meet them?' asked Frog.

A soft smile turned up the corners of her mouth, and Frog knew that it had been a long time since her face had felt such a smile. 'Do you have the key?'

Frog nodded and retrieved the key from his pouch. He held it up for her to see, and he noticed that his hand trembled, ever so slightly.

There was a low sigh from the figures around

them. It seemed to him that there was a sense of hope in the sound.

The woman turned away from Frog and raised her arms outwards. As her transparent form shifted, a breeze ruffled Frog's hair and passed through him. It travelled outwards and parted the dense mist, as if curtains were being drawn on a new day. The air cleared and the bright sky of daylight was revealed. Less than half a mile in front of them, tall granite cliffs stretched away into the distance on either side.

He turned to speak to Jorge and Mystra, and as he did so, the spectral figures dissolved into wispy trails of mist, and they vanished back into the thick, glutinous surface of the swamp.

They continued their journey towards the base of the cliffs in their own personal silence and thoughts, until the swamp came to an abrupt end and gave way to rocky ground, which became scattered with tangles of stunted, angry bushes. The sheer cliff wall towered over them; its height seemed to reach up into the very sky, where clusters of orange-tinted clouds nestled gently in both directions of its great length. A small stream flowed musically from a crack in the rocks to settle into a shallow pool, before it continued on its way down a narrow gully and out through the stony terrain.

'My brain feels that it's the middle of the night,' said Frog, as he shook his head in an effort to clear his senses.

'You two get a fire going,' said Jorge. 'I'll see what I can rustle up for food.'

Before either of them could caution him, he picked up his blowpipe and scrambled out of sight, over a large boulder.

In an attempt to keep the threat of sleep at bay, Frog knelt and splashed a handful of the cool stream water over his face, and Mystra joined him, cupping some of the liquid in her hands and taking a drink.

'It tastes sweet,' she remarked.

Frog leant forwards and gulped a mouthful straight out of the stream.

'You're right,' he replied. He was about to suggest that it tasted like flat lemonade, but he felt too tired to explain to Mystra what lemonade was.

By the time that he and Mystra had started a small fire, a grinning Jorge appeared clambering back over the boulders. He held aloft two cleaned and skinned rabbits.

They took the opportunity to fill their water bottles while the rabbits were cooking over the flames, and the smell brought back memories to Frog of the first time that he had awoken in the Dimension of Castellion, with Sir Peacealot sitting by an open fire, cooking a couple of rabbits in the same way. Frog tried to work out how long ago this had been, but his tired mind wouldn't allow him the concentration.

After they had eaten, they settled under the

shade of a craggy overhang, and with full stomachs, a drowsy sleep spread across their eyes. Each of them fell into a much needed, undisturbed slumber.

It was long into the day when the rattle of a small avalanche of rocks disturbed them from their dreamless rest. Frog got to his feet, blurry eyed and blinking as he grabbed his sword and stood with the others, who gazed upwards. The cause of the disturbance was a singular, aloof-looking mountain goat. It balanced precariously and almost impossibly like a tippy-toed ballerina on the sheer rock face a few metres above them.

As Frog's eyes became accustomed to the light, he noticed an enormous stone door carved into the rock face before them. It reached up at least four metres and was wide enough for the three of them to walk through alongside each other. It resembled an arched, gothic-style entrance to a church, except that there was no wood in its construction – the whole thing fitted seamlessly into the solid stone.

'That wasn't there before, was it?' he said to the others, with confused uncertainty.

22.

I Am the Chosen One

The door was perfect in every detail. The lines and texture of what should be wooden timber, the detail of the framework and the hinges that would normally be metal, were all carved in stone. There was a keyhole set to one side, but with no accompanying door handle.

Frog retrieved the key from his pouch and turned it over in his hand. 'If this doesn't fit, then I think that we're in trouble,' he joked.

No smiles crossed the faces of his companions.

'Okay. Here goes,' he said, as he inserted it into the keyhole. 'It won't turn,' he added as he tried to twist the key in both directions.

'Perhaps you've put it in the wrong way,' suggested Mystra. 'Take it out and try again.'

Frog tugged at the key. 'It's stuck,' he announced.

'Here, let me try,' said Jorge, stepping forwards.

Before he could place his hand on the key, its texture and form changed into stone, and it became moulded into the door.

'Oh, great! Now what?' Frog glanced at the others.

Slightly at first, the door began to vibrate. Small cracks zigzagged across its surface, like an expanding, misshapen spider web. Then, chunks of the stonework began to fall away as though the door was shedding a skin. The ground beneath their feet began to vibrate, and the three of them stepped backwards as discarded masonry fell away and crumbled into dust.

They watched, as an exact replica of the door was revealed, only now it was of dark, knotted wood. Heavy, black iron hinges supported it against a thick timbered framework, and after the dust settled, they could see that the key was now nestled in a stout metal lock, set below the large iron circle of a door handle.

'I'll try again,' said Frog, and he stepped forwards once more, and gripped the key. He twisted it anti-clockwise, and there was a loud resounding *click* from inside of the mechanism.

'Well,' said Mystra from over his shoulder. 'Open it.'

Frog turned the handle and gave the door a firm push. Without a noise of complaint from its hinges, it swung smoothly and silently inwards to reveal a long passageway, where emerald-tinted sunbeams streamed through an arched exit at the far end.

As the green light shimmered, Frog had a fleeting thought of *The Wizard of Oz*.

But, is this the Emerald City or the Witch's Castle? he mused to himself.

'Let's go,' said Mystra, rousing Frog out of his wonderings.

They grabbed their belongings and stepped through the open doorway.

'I'll just get this,' said Frog, as he retrieved the key and put it safely in his pouch to join the stone figure and the compass.

They had taken five or six paces into the passage, when the door swung closed and shut heavily behind them. Jorge went back to it, and in the semi-darkness, Frog heard him confirm what he and Mystra had already been thinking.

'There's no handle, no keyhole, and it won't move; we can't go back,' he announced.

'What a surprise,' said Frog.

It didn't take them long to travel the length of the passage, and as they reached the end, they realised that the green light was caused by the dappled reflections of leaf-covered branches, which overhung the exit.

They emerged into an open area of grass, surrounded by a wide ring of broad-leaved trees. As they stood taking in their surroundings, there was a grinding sound behind them, and alarmed, they turned to see that a seamless wall of solid rock now blocked the passageway.

'Someone doesn't want us to leave,' said Frog.

At the centre of the clearing was a large, grey stone. Veins of cobalt blue ran across its surface.

'It looks like an ancient altar stone,' remarked Mystra.

They moved forwards, the welcome sensation of warm sunlight caressed their faces, and helped to revive their energy and wash away the last damp traces of the swamp.

Frog stepped up to the stone block and ran his hand along the smooth surface; it somehow reminded him of the great monoliths that stood at Stonehenge.

'Frog?' It was Mystra's voice. She had been walking around and studying the entire oblong structure.

'What is it?'

'Have you seen the writing?'

He stepped down and followed the direction of her pointing finger.

'It starts here,' she prompted.

Carved into its sides was a message, and before he had worked his way around the stone, and finished digesting each word, he had guessed that this was another mystery of the Dimensions – it was a message that had been waiting just for him.

THIS STONE AWAITS A CHOSEN ONE
A GUARDIAN'S MESSENGER
A CHILD OF TERRAE
THE BLADE OF CASTELLION MUST PIERCE MY FORM
TO CALL TO ARMS THOSE WHO MUST DO THEIR DUTY.

It's a bit like the sword in the stone, but in reverse; instead of pulling out a blade, I've got to push mine in to prove who I am, he reasoned.

As Jorge and Mystra watched, he hauled himself up and onto the top of the stone; its plain, smooth surface was broken only by a symbol at its centre. As he stood upright, Frog looked down at the now familiar image of a burning sun, carved into the grey-blue rock.

'I'm not sure what's going to happen,' he said to the others. 'Usually I'm pulled into the Slipstream and I end up somewhere else, so if I disappear, it's not by my choice.'

He drew his sword from its scabbard; the blade glinted a hint of gold as he clasped his hands around the hilt and aimed the point down at the centre of the image.

As he raised his sword level with his eyes, ready to plunge it downwards, a deep voice echoed from within the surrounding trees.

'Hold! Move a feather's breadth and you will die where you stand.'

The tone of the voice, combined with his instinct, told Frog that the threat was deadly serious, and he froze. This was further confirmed when Mystra and Jorge reached for their blowpipes, and two black-feathered arrows flew from the bushes, and thudded into the ground at their feet.

'The next arrows let loose will hit their marks

and death will visit this hallowed place,' the same voice announced.

One thing that had not deserted Frog was his courage, and he spoke, loud and clear.

'I had heard that I might find brave warriors here, not cowards that skulk in the shadows.'

Another voice came; this time Frog detected a hint of curiosity.

'None may see us until the day of our calling. Now, you'd best do well and answer my questions. Who are you that desecrates the sacred stone?'

'He is the Chosen one,' explained Mystra.

'Silence, forest child!' the first voice boomed.

The second voice repeated the question. 'Who are you that desecrates the sacred stone?'

'I am Frog, sent by the Guardians of the Dimensions. I seek the Horsemen of Tropal.'

'You lie!' the deep voice accused. 'That lie shall cost you your life.'

'I'm not going to stand here and die without a fight,' yelled Jorge.

'Nor I,' shouted Mystra.

'No! Don't move,' pleaded Frog.

'You trespass into the Valley. You are forest children and evil has sent you to deceive us,' the deep voice continued.

'I *am* the Chosen one,' shouted Frog.

There was a murmur, a whispering of many voices from around the circle of trees.

'You lie!' The voice was deep and angry.

Frog instinctively knew that the moment had come when he had to take a chance.

'I AM THE CHOSEN ONE!' he shouted. He dropped to his knees and plunged the sword downwards. As its tip broke effortlessly through the surface of the stone, rays of bright yellow exploded outwards and filled the air with a dazzling light.

Frog felt the hilt of his sword vibrate so violently that he had to let go of it. A high-pitched tone began to resonate through the air. A single note, clear and high. The stone beneath him began to tremble and Frog rolled sideways, to fall and crouch on the ground beside Mystra and Jorge, who clasped their hands over their ears.

The musical note reached a high pitch and Frog pressed his own palms to his head in an effort to shut the piercing sound out. Against a wavering, blinding glare, he narrowed his eyes; he could just make out the shapes of numerous horses gathered around him.

The sound reached a climax, and just as Frog thought that it would shake the teeth from his gums, it stopped, leaving a silence that roared in his ears.

The bright light faded away and the three of them stood back-to-back, ready to fight, their eyes still blinking into focus as they awaited an uncertain future.

23.

The Horsemen of Tropal

Their vision slowly focussed to reveal the assembly of figures that now encircled them – the Horsemen of Tropal. However, these were no ordinary horsemen; none in the Valley had aged since the time of the Guardians curse, a curse that many, many years ago, had joined them to their steeds. Human and horse had become as one.

'Centaurs,' Frog whispered, in wonder.

The half men, half horses towered over them. Black. Chestnut. Pure white. Piebald. An array of glossy-coated, powerful steeds with the muscular upper bodies of men. Their torsos were criss-crossed with broad leather straps. Quivers of arrows were secured across their backs, to arm the powerfully strung bows in their hands, and large decorated, metal shields hung on their flanks.

Long flowing hair, which matched the colour of their coats, ran across their backs in splendid manes. The short stubble on their faces along with their strong jawlines and piercing dark eyes gave no doubt that these were a noble and fearsome people.

A centaur with jet-black flanks pushed forwards and trotted over to Frog's sword, which now stood upright, embedded into the ground, the stone no longer there, vanished. The centaur reached down and grasped the hilt. With one effortless pull, he raised the sword high into the air above him, like a trophy. For a moment, the blade rippled and shimmered with the gold-scripted writing of the ancient Guardians.

He moved towards Frog and brought the sword point level with the centre of Frog's chest. Without a word, both Jorge and Mystra pushed Frog back and placed themselves protectively in front of him; their colours blazed and rippled in defiance.

Around them, bowstrings tightened, and a myriad of arrows were aimed to deliver certain death. In the following anxious moments, the centaur studied them as if deciding their fate, until his deep, resonant voice broke the silence.

'Let him step forwards. He must complete the test.'

'What more proof do you need?' asked Mystra.

'This?' The centaur nodded at the sword. 'Any fool could have stolen this.' His brow furrowed and Mystra could see a dark resolve in his eyes. 'Now, move aside or you shall all die here and none shall be the wiser.'

Frog gently eased Mystra and Jorge aside.

'No one has to die here,' he said. 'What is it that you want of me?'

The centaur lowered the blade, and leaned to whisper into Frog's ear. Frog smiled a knowing look at him, and whispered back.

The centaur's expression softened, and with a flick of his wrist, he flipped the sword around and presented it back to Frog.

'I am honoured to return your sword,' he said. Then he turned and addressed the gathered group. 'Hear me, one and all. The time of our judgement is at hand. He *is* the Chosen one.'

The bows were lowered, and in salute, all of the centaurs clenched their fists to their chests. Their hooves struck the ground in unison, building up a strong rhythm until it reached a thunderous crescendo, which then ended in a sudden and dramatic echo.

Mystra leant forwards and spoke into Frog's ear. 'What did he ask you?'

'He wanted to know my real name – my earth name,' he smiled.

The centaur spoke. 'I am Dagar, and this is my son, Victor.'

A chestnut-coloured centaur moved alongside him. His face had gentler lines and features, but Frog could see that there was a brooding strength also in his eyes.

'These are my companions, Mystra and Jorge,' said Frog.

'They are loyal and brave,' said Dagar. 'And they would surely lay down their lives for you.'

'And I for them,' added Frog.

Dagar held out an open hand. 'Come. We must make haste; before this day is ended, there shall be a gathering of all our people. You ride with me.'

Frog took the outstretched hand and was lifted up, as if he were nothing more than a sack of feathers, onto the centaur's back. He sat there unsteadily as Mystra and Jorge were helped up onto two other centaurs.

'Hold on. I wouldn't want you falling off and breaking your neck.' The centaur grinned.

'What do people usually hang on to?' Frog asked, nervously.

'No one has ever been allowed to ride on us before, so I would suggest that you grasp my straps. However, don't even think of pulling my hair,' he glared.

The company of centaurs pushed their way through the bushes and trees, and out into the flat landscape of a wide valley where a river wound its way into the distance like a silver thread, and the land was fertile and green. Trees were sparsely populated, and nowhere near as abundant as the forests of Tropal.

'We have a long ride ahead of us,' said Dagar.

'If you need to rest at any time, let me know. Messengers have already left to send word of your coming, so by the time we get there, preparations will be well underway.'

'Preparations for what?'

'For a gathering, to bring together all those who were exiled to this valley. We have long awaited this day, and of when we shall be told of the hour of our release.'

'You were waiting for us,' said Frog. 'How did you know that we were coming?'

'Just because we are imprisoned in the Valley,' said Dagar. 'Does not mean that we do not know what transpires outside.'

Frog was intrigued. 'How?'

Dagar looked upwards. 'There is one that watches for us.'

Frog followed his gaze and saw the silhouette of a large-winged bird, an eagle, as it circled effortlessly in the thermals overhead.

'So, how much do you know?' asked Frog.

'Save your questions my young friend. The time of our release is near. Now it is time to chase the wind. To home and the gathering. Hold on tight!' he shouted.

Dagar reared up and kicked out with his front legs, his hooves cartwheeled in the air, and Frog grasped the leather straps, which crossed the centaur's broad shoulders.

Then they were off, Centaurs galloping out across the valley, heads high, manes and tails flying like triumphant flags.

Frog was grateful that he had gained some experience of riding from when he had his own horse, Thunder, back in Castellion. Once more, this prompted memories to fill his head of where his travels had taken him. He wondered about Lady Dawnstar and his other friends that he had left behind in the medieval world. Visions of people and places from both Castellion and the second Dimension of Aridian swept through his mind. He smiled as he recalled familiar faces, and remembered sadly those who had been lost helping him to fight against the evil of Lord Maelstrom.

Will this be the final quest? he wondered. *Will it all end here, and will I ever get home again?*

He didn't know how long he had been immersed in his thoughts. Daydreaming, his eyes had been open to the journey, but had seen nothing. He became aware that it had become cooler and darker, as if a cloud had covered the sun on a warm summer's day.

It was Mystra's voice that brought his senses fully awake.

'Look! In the sky,' she cried out her warning.

Dagar and the others brought themselves to a halt. All followed the direction of Mystra's pointing finger.

A large, black, foreboding cloud had formed high above them. It swirled and billowed with the threat of an oncoming storm. Then, from its spiralling centre emerged an enormous, dark-winged shape. Even before crimson-orange flames flared out in scorching jets of death from its nostrils, Frog knew what the beast was.

'A black dragon,' he murmured.

In that moment, and even at a great distance, the creature's blood-red eyes locked onto Frog. It seemed to pick him out, as a falcon would home in on its prey. It spread its leathery wings and beat the air in malicious rage, and its great bulk hovered as if to defy gravity. It let out a thunderous roar and released two long streams of burning destruction.

A guttural voice invaded Frog's head. *I know that you speak the language of dragons. You cannot shield yourself from me, and these puny fools cannot protect you. All those that stand in my way shall perish, and I will feel your soft flesh tear in my claws as I take you to my master.*

Frog tore his eyes away from the beast. 'Run for cover,' he warned. 'We need to find shelter.'

He looked around him, frantically seeking for a safe haven. They were trapped in the open; the valley cliffs were at least a mile away on either side of them. The dragon would descend and incinerate them all before they covered even half of the distance. In a desperate moment to protect the others, he shouted, 'There's no need for you all to die. It's me that it's after. Leave me here, and run.'

Dagar spoke to Frog. 'Do you think that would satisfy his master? Do you really think that we would be spared? No. Such evil does not spare life when it is there for the taking.' He turned to the others. 'We stand and fight. Spread out and sound the horns.'

Three centaurs produced ornately carved white horns, and placed them to their lips. The sound produced was loud and brassy, like that of trumpets. Two notes, one high, one low, were repeated several times, until they echoed away across the Valley.

Above them, the dragon folded its wings in against its scaly body, and it fell like a giant black arrow towards them; its forked tail flailed out behind it, and a furnace of fire raged in its throat ready to burn them all into oblivion.

'The three of you, get onto the ground,' instructed Dagar.

Frog, Mystra and Jorge dismounted. Frog drew his sword, ever optimistic that he would somehow get the opportunity to use it on the beast.

'Lie on the ground,' said Dagar. 'For what protection it may offer, we will cover you with our shields.'

'I'd rather stand and fight,' protested Frog.

'And I would rather you had a chance of survival,' said Dagar. 'Now cover yourselves with our shields.'

Frog stood firm as Dagar's eyes locked onto his.

'Cover yourselves with the shields,' he repeated. 'That is *not* a request.'

The bulk of the dragon loomed larger by the second, and Frog knew from experience that the creature would suddenly spread out its enormous wings and flap them in great sweeping movements. It would hover as it gushed long jets of fire at them, and fan the flames to spread the furnace over as much ground as possible.

Mystra turned to Frog. 'You know that we have to protect you at all costs.'

Frog pursed his lips. 'Okay,' he said, with resignation. 'But we stay together. Right?'

Shields were handed down to them, and they hastily built a shell-like covering, and crawled into it.

The centaurs formed a long line, and loaded up their bows, their arrows aimed skywards.

'When I give the order,' shouted Dagar, 'fire the first volley at its head. Maybe we'll get lucky and hit an eye or send one down its throat. On the second command aim at its belly where the skin is soft.'

For a moment, all that Frog could hear was an eerie silence. Then the unmistakable sound of rushing air vibrated the shields around them – the great beast was hovering, ready to deliver its fiery assault.

'Fire!' Dagar's voice boomed the order. Twenty-four arrows swished into the air, followed by a thunderous roar from the dragon. 'Fire!' A second command rang out from Dagar.

More arrows flew skywards, to herald another ear-splitting roar from the beast. The horns trumpeted their two-note alarm, and the ground trembled from the force of many scattering hooves. A blast of fire turned a swathe of ground black and charcoaled, and it swept over the heap of shields. Crouched in their metal cocoon, Frog, Jorge and Mystra gasped as the air around them heated up like an oven.

'I'm not going to be roasted to death,' Frog shouted defiantly. 'I'll take my chances out there.' He threw back a scorched shield, and as his arm touched the metal, his skin blistered. Mystra and Jorge followed suit, and hot steel also left angry, red burns across their arms as the shields tumbled away.

Already, the fight was not without casualties. Frog observed several fallen bodies strewn around, and he had to look away as some of them were scorched and charred beyond recognition.

Blackened patches of seared grass smoked like funeral pyres around them. Centaurs aimed their bows upward, now seemingly hesitant to fire their arrows. The air was rent with a snarling howl; this time there was fear in the sound, and Frog looked up to see the dragon besieged by a horde of what he could only take in as centaurs with wings – half human, half Pegasus. These were the women – the wives and daughters of the Horsemen. The Guardian had also transformed them as punishment.

They attacked the dragon with swords and spears and shredded one of the creature's wings to such an extent that it became ripped and tattered. With a final, hopeless flail, the dragon spiralled aimlessly to the ground.

The creature hit the earth with a resounding impact, and it thrashed out in violent defence as the winged centaurs hovered overhead to send a flurry of arrows at its head and body. Frog felt the stirrings of pity for the animal, which were immediately cut short as one of its blood-red eyes focussed on him, and its voice reached into Frog's mind.

My brethren exist in all worlds, even in your Dimension. My master shall awaken them to carry out his bidding. Even now, your loved ones are being sought out and he will ensure that you never see them again.

The words chilled his very bones, and Frog watched without compassion as every able centaur besieged the dragon. Their weapons showed no mercy; until with one last fragile roar, its great bulk moved no more.

'I have never seen such a creature before,' said Jorge.

Frog didn't hear him; his mind was focussed on images of his parents. Terrible images of their faces wracked with pain. He began to shake as he realised that somehow Lord Maelstrom's influence had reached into the one place that he thought would be safe – his own Dimension. His home.

'Frog? Frog!' Jorge's voice jolted him back to the present.

Frog gasped a sharp intake of breath. 'I've got to go,' he said in a panic. 'I've got to get home. My parents are in danger!' He raised his sword, to thrust it into the earth and to open up the Slipstream.

'Stop him!' warned Mystra. 'The Guardian told me that if Frog returned to his home, if the Slipstream takes him, then all could be lost. No, Frog!' she screamed. 'Stop!'

Oblivious to her pleas, Frog plunged his sword towards the ground.

24.

PARALLEL

A full moon shone its celestial light down on the grass and trees of a small orchard. The air was motionless with a breathless, summer night – a night when hunters crept in the shadows and hedgerows.

The shape of a fox paused beneath the trees. With a sniff, she raised her snout; her senses worked like fine-tuned antennae. The hairs on her burnished brown coat bristled slightly. Something was about to disturb her business. Something from the realms of secret mysteries. She paused, half hidden in the shadows, interested to see what or who was using magic in her domain.

Beneath the lush leaves and ripening fruit of the trees, a patch of air shimmered and swirled. Ripples formed as though the air had become liquid. Then a dark circle opened, and expanded to reveal a velvet curtain strewn with white and blue star points.

The shape of a curled-up human form slipped

through its centre and fell softly to the ground like a discarded bundle of clothes. As the Slipstream sealed its secret doorway, blades of grass shifted gently against the traveller's face and prickled his senses awake. He rolled over onto his back and inhaled a breath of midnight air.

The fox did not run; she sat comfortably on her haunches, her bushy tail wrapped around her, and her head cocked to one side as she observed the scene from her unseen place.

The figure sat himself upright, his head cleared as he breathed in the humid air, and he looked around at his surroundings. The trees stood in their summer elegance like dark sentinels. Moonlight made the stems of grass seem as though they were coated in thousands of tiny jewels.

He pulled back the hood of his cloak, and the thick material settled in folds around his neck. Through a gap in the trees, he could see the large, black shape of a house, a familiar house, and one that he had visited before. For a moment, he sat and listened to the night's silence.

'I know you are there,' he spoke quietly. 'You can come out now.'

The fox uncurled her tail, and wandered confidently from the shade until she sat facing the man. They studied each other, allowing their eyes to meet only for a fleeting second.

From the undergrowth, other eyes looked on in

deliberate silence – they watched with hatred and desires of evil cunning.

'It is not often that your kind walks this earth,' the fox spoke; her voice as smooth and soft as velvet. 'And I sense that you are no stranger to this place.'

'That's true.' The man smiled.

'I am the Watcher of this place,' said the fox. 'I have a duty of vigilance on this house, and those who live here.' She cocked her head towards the sleeping building. 'But you already knew that, didn't you?'

'I sense that we share the same magic, you and I,' said the man. 'The magic of the Slipstream.'

'Then your presence here must be of great importance,' said the fox. 'Tell me all that I need to know. Begin with your name.'

'My name is Logan. An ancient evil is stirring in this world. The Slipstream has created a time shift, a parallel, a duality; the boy is here, in your time, but at this very moment, he also exists in the Dimension of Tropal, where his courage is being tested. If he departs that place before his task is complete, time will collapse and all will be lost. I am here to deliver a message, to let him know that we protect his loved ones across the Dimensions.'

'You are a long way from home, Logan,' said the fox.

'I am from the Dimension of Castellion. In the past, the boy and I fought beside each other. I am honoured to call him a true friend.'

The fox nodded her head, thoughtfully. 'He sleeps,' she said.

'Then it is now that I need to deliver my message,' said Logan. 'I bid you good hunting.' He tapped his forehead in a farewell salute, and strode quietly towards the house.

Logan was bestowed with the gift of unrestricted access. No door, no gate, no window, no entrance or exit of any kind could prevent him from passing through. All barriers and locks would open for him, and so it was that he found himself in Chris' bedroom. He stood silently over the sleeping boy.

He allowed himself a smile of recognition at his young friend, and then he spoke quietly in the language of the Guardians. Chris would not hear the words that fell from Logan's lips until the time that they were needed, although the man's image would skirt the back of Chris' mind like an elusive dream.

Logan left the house as silently as an old memory, leaving locked doors behind him. He made his way back to the orchard, and found the fox still there.

'I thought that you had hunting to attend to,' he said as he approached the animal.

'I also have the duty of watching,' replied the fox. 'We are not the only ones that have an interest in the house this night.'

Logan looked down at the black oily-furred animal, which squirmed and wriggled to escape from beneath the weight of the fox's paw, a paw that was firmly placed on the back of the creature's neck.

'I see you have caught yourself a meal,' he said.

'I wouldn't eat this wretched thing,' said the fox. 'Its taste would be as rancid as the wickedness that it serves.'

Logan crouched down for a closer look at the animal: a rat. Its yellow teeth snapped and it threw out a venomous hiss in an attempt to reach him.

'This despicable animal is a messenger, a sneak, a stealer of knowledge and secrets, and when commanded, it is also capable of most dreadful deeds,' said the fox. 'Its eyes and ears are windows to the evil one. At the moment, it works alone, but there are other terrible, ancient things that sleep in the earth, waiting for when the dark power is strong enough to reach them and release them.'

It was then that the rat spoke in a deep rasping voice, unnatural for its size. 'My master is coming, and you cannot stop him. You are doomed and there is nothing that you can do.'

'Oh, I believe there is,' said the fox. She picked the rat up by its neck, and held it between her teeth. Logan guessed what was about to happen, and he looked away. There was a loud, high-pitched squeal followed by the muffled crack of breaking bones. He turned back just as the animal's discarded body landed limp and lifeless amongst some nearby bushes.

'Was that really necessary?' he asked. 'After all, it was just a rat.'

'Pure evil comes in all shapes and sizes, Logan. When that evil wants to kill everything that is good, decent, and kind, when it threatens my family, then I will do anything that is necessary to stop it.'

Logan raised an eyebrow. 'Your family?'

The fox ignored the question and sniffed at the air. 'Have you carried out your task?'

He studied the fox for a moment. 'I have placed a message into his subconscious that will strengthen his courage. It will expose the lies that the evil one will try to poison his mind with, lies about the safety of his family. I have fulfilled my purpose here.'

'Then it is time for you to go, lest Gizmo becomes impatient with your absence,' she said.

Surprise lit up on Logan's face. 'You know of Gizmo, the Guardian of Castellion?'

'There are many things that I know, and many things that I do not know,' said the fox. 'That is the way of things.'

The rippled vortex of the Slipstream appeared behind Logan.

'I believe that you are more than a Watcher,' he said.

'We are all more than we seem to be. I am sure that we shall meet again, Logan.'

As his body was enveloped in the whirling current of the Slipstream, Logan's last conscious image was that of the fox's deep amber eyes.

25.

VALLEY OF THE HORSEMEN

In the darkness, Frog heard Logan's voice. He heard his words, which pushed back any fear and doubt in his mind. It was as though a suffocating shroud had been pulled back from his senses, and he knew now that his parents were safe and being watched over. In that moment, all panic left him.

His eyelids fluttered open, and slowly his blurred vision cleared to reveal concerned faces staring down at him, two of them with shifting, deep-pastel colours on their skin.

'Here, drink this,' said Mystra, and she brought a flask of water to his lips.

As he sipped at the welcome liquid, he became aware that he was propped up on her knees. His head throbbed with a sharp pain, and he tentatively brought his hand up to feel a tender lump beneath his dishevelled hair.

'Sorry about that,' said Dagar. 'It was the only way that I could stop you.'

Realisation dawned on a still dazed Frog. 'You kicked me?'

'Just a glancing blow, otherwise you would not be alive to have this conversation.'

'Remind me not to stand behind you again!'

'We couldn't let you leave,' said Jorge. 'Our Guardian told us that if you opened up the Slipstream and left us, we might never get you back – time would change.'

'It was my own fault,' admitted Frog. 'I let my guard down. Even now, I still underestimate Lord...' He stopped himself. 'The evil one's powers. He got inside of my head. Thanks to a few words from an old friend of mine called Logan, I can see the truth now.'

'Here,' said Dagar. He tossed a small leather bag to Mystra. 'Apply some of this salve to his head; it will help with the healing and stop the pain.'

As Mystra gently rubbed some of the soft paste onto his head, he winced slightly. The soothing effect of the salve began to spread, and Frog relaxed further into Mystra's lap as he inwardly smiled to himself, enjoying her attention.

I seem to make a habit of this, he thought, and he remembered the moments when Fixer and Nadiah, the girls in the other Dimensions, had tended to him when he had sustained previous injuries.

'All done,' she announced. 'I think that you should try to stand now.' Frog noticed a sudden change in the tone of her voice, as though she were annoyed at him.

'Come on, my friend,' said Jorge as he grasped Frog's hands. 'Up you come.'

The upward movement gave Frog a slight head-rush, and he wobbled unsteadily.

'It's okay.' He blinked, and he took in a deep breath.

Mystra passed the pouch back to Dagar, and then she looked sternly at Frog. 'Who are Fixer and Nadiah?' she asked.

Frog sensed a hint of jealousy in her voice. 'Just some friends from the other Dimensions.'

'I got the impression that they were more than just friends.'

'Were you looking into my thoughts?' Frog smiled.

'I… I didn't mean to,' she responded with slight embarrassment. 'You sort of opened your guard and I caught a brief glimpse of them.'

'They were very close friends, who I grew fond of. Just as I have grown fond of you.'

She gave him a wide smile. Despite his best efforts, he blushed at her.

'It may all seem very nice, but we haven't got time to stand around like this,' interrupted Dagar. 'With danger about, we need to get moving.'

Frog looked around. The winged women now stood amongst the centaurs. Many had open and bloody wounds on their bodies. One of them, with a gold breastplate strapped on her body, stood next to Dagar. Her white mane was stained with fresh red, dragon's blood.

'This is Locrin, my wife and leader of our flying women,' introduced Dagar. 'I think it would be wise if they transported you for the rest of your journey. It will be quicker and safer.'

'You mean fly on their backs?' said Mystra; her eyes were wide with excitement.

'Certainly,' said Locrin. 'I hope that you have a head for heights.'

'No problem,' said Frog. 'After all, I have flown with dragons,' he boasted.

As soon as the words came out of his mouth, he realised that it was not the right time to say such a thing. Many hooves stamped the ground, and he caught an angry murmur pass through those who had heard.

Locrin loomed over him. 'I have just lost many friends defeating that beast, and now you say that you ride with them?' she growled. 'Give me one good reason why I should not crush your skull beneath my hooves.'

Frog looked at Dagar, who stared back darkly, and then he looked back to face Locrin.

'No. No! Not with the black dragons. Not all dragons are like them. I have a kinship with the Dragon Riders of Castellion, and with the most loyal dragons that you could wish to meet,' he said, hurriedly. 'I am sure that if they existed in this Dimension, they would come to your aid and fight alongside you. If I have offended you, I apologise and I offer every respect to those who have laid down their lives in protecting me.' He knelt and bowed his head before Locrin.

There was an unnerving silence, until Locrin spoke.

'Stand. We are all foolish with words from time to time. It is putting right the offence that matters. Apology accepted. Now, you ride with me and I shall show you flying the like of which no dragon can match.'

★★★

Just before night fell with its regular suddenness, they landed in the village compound. Frog was breathless with exhilaration and fear. Locrin was right: flying with her was totally different to flying with dragons. To say that it was better would be wrong.

Reckless – Yes. Dangerous – Yes. Exciting – Yes. An honour – Yes.

However, Frog would not say that it was better, and he had to use all of his diplomatic skills when Locrin asked him how it compared.

'Awesome!' he exclaimed. 'I have never experienced anything like it.' Thankfully, this satisfied Locrin.

Frog reflected afterwards how easily he had offended the Horsemen and Horsewomen, and how he continued to learn that it was always better to engage his brain before he opened his mouth!

Flaming torches illuminated the village, which consisted of a mixture of wooden stables and round, straw-roofed huts. Frog, Jorge and Mystra dismounted, and from the buildings around them came a stream of boys and girls, who welcomed the Horsewomen with kisses and affectionate pats. The children of the Horsemen's population had been spared the curse of the Guardian, and had remained in human form and unaffected. Frog thought how distressing it must have been for them when their parents had been transformed.

Now, at a time of welcoming, the mood quickly changed when it became apparent that there were several Horsewomen missing – fatal casualties of the dragon's fire.

A shroud of mourning quickly settled over the community, and as many of the wounded were taken to the stables to be tended to, Locrin took Frog and his companions to a dwelling at the edge of the compound.

A girl in her early teens, with long, dark hair and a gentle face, waited patiently at the door, until, overcome by joy, she ran forwards and threw her arms around Locrin.

'This is my daughter, Janine. You are our guests. Our house is your house.'

'Where is Father?' asked Janine, as concern crept across her face.

'He will be here soon. We had to fight one of the foulest creatures imaginable, but do not worry; he is safe.'

Relief brightened Janine's eyes.

'This is Frog, Mystra and Jorge,' said Locrin. 'Frog is a very special person,' she smiled. 'He is the Chosen one of Legend.'

For a moment, Janine studied Frog. She looked up to her mother. 'Is it true? Will the curse finally be lifted from you? Is he really the one? Our salvation?'

'For our sakes, I believe that he is,' replied Locrin. 'Now I must bid you goodnight,' she said to them all. 'I must go and comfort those who have lost loved ones.'

She kissed her daughter tenderly on the head, and trotted silently away.

Janine welcomed them into the hut, and showed them to three simple straw beds. 'I hope that you will be comfortable,' she said. 'I will prepare some food for us.'

Presently, they sat outside around a small fire. There was very little conversation, as Janine seemed slightly in awe of her company, particularly of Frog, whom she kept shyly glancing at. It was after a plain, but welcome meal that they exchanged their goodnight wishes. Janine left to join her parents elsewhere in the village. A single beeswax candle gently flickered soothing shadows around the hut, as the three companions settled down on soft beds.

'What a day,' said Mystra. 'I never thought that I would fly like that.'

'Nor I,' said Jorge. 'What say you, Frog?'

The silence was broken by the hushed snore of restful sleep, which floated from Frog's slumbering shape.

26.

The Parting of Friends

The crowing of a cockerel roused them, and as they rubbed the traces of sleep from their eyes, the aroma of freshly baked bread drifted into the hut and awakened their senses. Janine came in with a smile and a morning greeting.

'There is a stream behind the hut for you to wash away the night and refresh yourselves, and I have breakfast cooking on the fire. I hope that you like fresh eggs and bread.'

Outside, Frog stretched his arms and legs, and gave a short yawn as he breathed in the already warm and clear morning air. He looked at the distant purple-tipped mountains that secured the Valley and imprisoned the village, and he wondered what events were unfolding beyond their peaks, in this Dimension and in others beyond the Slipstream.

He wandered along a narrow track and down a small incline to a wide stream, which collected into a large pool; its liquid surface shifted in silver swirls and eddies before it flowed gently away over scattered rocks. As he stood on the bank and listened to the watery soundtrack, Logan's message echoed quietly again in his head. *Your loved ones are safe. They are protected. The Light exists in time and space, wherever evil threatens, and it guards us all. Find the Tree of Spells, restore peace to the Dimensions, and put an end to Lord Maelstrom.*

Frog smiled as he remembered Logan – the man's jet-black hair, the white scar that ran down the side of his face, and the red eye patch with an eye stencilled into the leather. He was a fearsome sight, and one of the most loyal friends that Frog had encountered on his journeys through the Dimensions.

I wonder if we'll meet again, my friend, thought Frog.

'Are you going to stand there all day admiring the view?' Mystra's voice interrupted his thoughts.

'Just remembering an old friend,' said Frog.

'Living or dead?' she asked.

'Very much alive, I believe.'

'Well, I hope that he's got more energy than you. You're still half asleep. Come on,' she said, with a smile. 'Let's go for a swim!'

Frog noticed a mischievous gleam in her eyes just before she gave him a gentle shove; it was enough to send him off balance and tumbling headfirst into the pool. The cold water shocked his senses fully awake. He broke through the surface, to stand submerged up to his shoulders, coughing and spluttering.

'Right!' he shouted as he waded towards Mystra, who stood on the bank, grinning. 'You're going to pay for that.'

'I'll save you the trouble,' she laughed, and she dived over his head and into the water.

A vigorous water fight followed with much splashing, shouting and screaming. Mystra's colours rippled and swirled in delight as Frog caught her, lifted her up and dunked her in the now foaming and bubbling pool. When she surfaced, she was facing him and they both breathed heavily with excitement. For a moment, all was still as they looked into each other's eyes. Frog felt a familiar twinge, a fluttering in his stomach.

'Hey! What's all the shouting?' Jorge appeared at the edge of the pool.

A broad smile spread across Mystra's face. She kissed the tip of Frog's nose, and then slipped beneath the surface like a playful mermaid.

'You'd better hurry up and get dried,' said Jorge. 'Breakfast is nearly ready.' He knelt down and splashed some clean water across his face and neck. 'Brrr!' he exclaimed. 'Too cold for me at the moment.'

Frog looked on as Mystra surfaced and made her way to the bank.

'Frog? Are you alright?' asked Jorge.

'Sure. Sure,' replied Frog, as he brought his senses back from their wanderings, and waded out of the pool.

It wasn't long before they sat around a small fire outside of the hut, Janine having served up a tasty breakfast of fried eggs and mushrooms. They had eagerly soaked up the last of the juices from their plates with pieces of fresh bread.

'That was delicious,' commented Frog.

Jorge and Mystra agreed, and all three of them gratefully thanked Janine. They offered to wash up the plates and pots, but Janine would have none of it.

'At least let us help you to clear up,' said Mystra.

'Very well,' replied Janine. 'You can help me to carry them down to the stream, but that is all.'

Just as they were about to leave, Dagar arrived and bid them a good morning.

'Frog, I need to speak with you.'

'We were just going to help Janine,' said Mystra.

'That's alright,' he said. 'It is Frog who I need to speak to, alone. You and Jorge may go with Janine.'

Jorge and Mystra exchanged glances of curiosity before they followed Janine towards the stream.

Dagar waited patiently until they were out of sight. 'You must make a decision, my young friend. One of your companions is to stay with us until the time of our freedom.'

'I thought that the Guardian wanted them both to stay with me,' said Frog.

Dagar stamped a hoof, and his tail gave an agitated swish. 'We have lived under the curse of the Guardian for too long; now comes the time of our redemption. As a token of trust, one of you must stay until we are free from the Guardian's spell.'

'It sounds as if you want to keep one of us captive,' stated Frog.

'It is about trust,' insisted Dagar. 'When we ride out of our own captivity and into freedom, so shall they.'

'I still have to find the Tree of Spells. I may need them both to help me.'

Dagar leant forwards, his face towered centimetres from Frog's face. 'You are the Chosen one. You should need no help. Decide.'

Even though there was a smile on Dagar's face, Frog sensed an air of menace in his voice. For now, he had no choice. He had to trust him.

'Name who is to stay,' said Dagar.

'Jorge,' announced Frog, without a second thought. 'But let me be the one to tell him.'

'Of course. Now, I have something for you. Something that was left in my care when the Valley was sealed.' Dagar produced a small, rolled-up piece of light-brown leather. It was bound by a strip of black twine, which in turn was sealed with a lump of blood-red candle wax. Melted into the wax was the sign of the Chosen – a burning sun.

Frog took it and turned it over in his hands. There was something small wrapped inside it.

'I think that I'll open it when the others return,' he said, and he put it into his pouch.

'I sense that you are wary of me, young Frog.'

Frog stood his ground and looked straight at Dagar. 'I have learnt on my travels that things are not always as they seem to be. Also that the evil of the Dark Lord can make enemies out of those who you regard as friends.'

'You are wise beyond your years,' said Dagar. 'Let us hope that your wisdom will protect us *all* from the evil lord.'

As much as Frog wanted to trust Dagar, it still troubled him whether or not the Horsemen would come to the help of Tropal when they were needed.

'When you have read your message, let me know how I can help with the next step of your quest,' said Dagar. 'I go now to ceremony, and to bid farewell to slain friends. I will return this afternoon to discuss your plans.'

After Dagar had gone, Frog sat himself in the hut and emptied his pouch. He studied the clues – the small figure, the compass, and the key. He decided to open the leather package before the others returned. As gently as he could, he broke away the wax seal, and as luck would have it, he managed to keep it in one piece. He picked apart a single knot in the twine, and unfolded the square of leather.

'Well. What a surprise. Another clue,' he said to himself, sarcastically.

Nestling in the centre of the material was a glass crystal, about the size of his thumb. As he examined it, tiny reflections of his face stared back at him, and prisms of light glinted like small sparks of energy.

There was also a message written into the leather with black ink. Its thin and scrawny lettering was just decipherable.

BY THE LIGHT OF THE MOON
AT BLACK MOUNTAIN'S GATE
MY WINDOWS SHALL REVEAL TWO PATHS
ONE TO WHAT YOU SEEK
THE OTHER TO OBLIVION
WHICH ONE TO TAKE SHALL BE PLAIN TO SEE.

He was still studying the crystal, when he heard the others return. Mystra came into the hut, followed by Jorge.

She sat next to Frog. 'What have you got there?'

'It's another clue. Dagar gave it to me.'

'What's it say?' asked Jorge.

'We'll talk about that in a minute,' said Frog. 'Sit down. I've got something to tell you.'

Jorge looked at Frog. 'You've got your serious face on. Better do as I'm told,' he joked.

Frog told them about his conversation with Dagar, and how he had decided that Jorge was to be the one to stay with the Horsemen.

'Sounds good to me,' said Jorge.

'You mean, you don't mind?' said Frog.

'Are you kidding? I get to ride and fly with them, while you two wander around aimlessly to goodness knows where, looking for more clues,' Jorge replied.

Frog still sensed a hint of disappointment in Jorge's voice.

'What do *you* think?' Frog asked Mystra, who had remained silent.

'I would prefer that we all stick together, but it has to be your decision, and we have to accept that as long as it is for the right reason.' She studied Frog's eyes for a moment, and before he could respond, she continued. 'Now, let's have a look at this new clue.'

Frog gave the crystal to Mystra, and he handed the piece of leather to Jorge.

Jorge took in a sharp breath. 'Black Mountain! You don't want to go anywhere near Black Mountain.'

The colours paled from Mystra's face. 'Why do we have to go to Black Mountain? There's only death waiting there.'

Frog took in a deep breath. 'I must follow the clues, and if there is any chance that Mystra and I can rescue any of the captives, then all the more reason for us to go there. If we don't face our fears, we may as well give up.'

'It's where the evil one is hiding out,' said Jorge. 'It's also where he takes his captives and drains the colours from them.' To reflect this, his face was now grey and saddened.

A single tear trickled down Mystra's cheek, and it hung like a raindrop from her chin. 'You're right,' she sniffed. 'I forget that there are so many depending on us.'

She turned and looked at Frog. 'Don't you ever get afraid of what might happen to you?'

'Of course.' Frog wiped the tear away with his thumb. 'Sometimes I wonder, *Why me?* Sometimes I feel like running away and going home, just to forget about the Dimensions and to be with my family and my friends. Then I remember what *he* can do, and that eventually he will destroy everything and everyone who I love if I don't at least try to stop him.'

Mystra looked at Jorge. 'Black Mountain is my destiny, then,' she said.

Later in the day, Dagar and Locrin came to the

202

hut, and in the warm, afternoon air, Frog showed them the crystal and the clue. Neither Dagar nor Locrin mentioned Black Mountain, but Frog noticed a flicker of concern pass between them as they read the words.

'I can take you as far as Glacier Pass,' said Locrin. 'It's at the far end of the Valley and high in the foothills. There is a gateway spell, which prevents any of us from leaving, but from there you will be able to see your destination, and nothing should block *your* way out.'

'The temperature drops so suddenly at night that many creatures have become trapped and frozen in the ice over the years,' said Dagar.

'Sounds like we'll be needing warmer clothes,' said Frog.

'Don't worry, we will make sure that you have supplies and something to protect you from the daytime cold,' he said.

'When can we leave?' asked Frog.

'It is best to set out at daybreak,' said Locrin. 'I can get you to the pass by midday, and that will give you enough time to cross the glacier before nightfall.'

'Tomorrow at daybreak it is, then,' said Frog.

'Tonight there will be a celebration of the lives lost in battle, and you shall all join us as guests,' said Dagar.

After night had fallen and golden sparks

floated upwards into the ink-black sky, carried by the heat from a large raging bonfire, Frog and the others were seated at a low wooden table. They watched as the names of the fallen were read out with great ceremony, and they gasped in wonder and amazement at the spectacular acrobatics and dangerous swordplay that the Horsemen and Horsewomen enacted in honour of their lost comrades.

The next morning with images of the previous evening still drifting across their thoughts, Frog and Mystra, both of them feeling uncomfortably warm in their thick clothing, prepared to climb onto Locrin's broad back. Frog shook Jorge's hand, and told him to keep out of harm's way. 'Till we meet again, my friend. I'll look for you in my mind as often as I can,' Frog promised.

Mystra gave Jorge a lengthy hug, until she finally let him go with a kiss on his cheek.

With a stamp of Locrin's hooves and a beating of wings, they were lifted into the air. Mystra, seated behind him, hugged Frog's waist and was unaware of the broad grin on his face.

'Here's to your success,' shouted Dagar. 'If all is well, we shall see you in battle.'

As they rose into the sky, Frog carried with him a still nagging doubt. *When the time comes, will the Horsemen of Tropal honour their pledge?*

27.

ASSAULT ON THE CANOPY

In the distance, Lord Maelstrom's spies, their shrivelled hearts full of his dark hate, searched the horizon with their cold, black eyes.

He had invaded the mountain's forgotten tunnels and caverns, and scoured the shadows of long-buried places; it was there that he had awakened an ancient magic, which he greedily consumed to strengthen his powers and to feed his evil hunger. His form and shape took on a new and terrible appearance: a shifting cloak of tomb-black and blood red vapour surrounded him – a living garment of poison and malice.

Deep within Black Mountain, he strode along its rock-hewn and liquid-glistening corridors. He busied himself with unspeakable evil, and created the twisted monsters of his new soulless army. When the time was ready, he would release them to spread death and desolation. He would become all-powerful; no force in all the known worlds and

Dimensions would be able to defeat him. Time itself would bow down at his feet, darkness would befall all, and in that darkness, he would rule for eternity.

'Let us begin to put their resolve to the test,' he announced to the writhing darkness at his feet.

Since he had first created the Drak, they had captured hundreds of Tropal's children, and as Frog and Mystra journeyed far away on the wings of Locrin, a ghostly army of colourless figures spilled out from the foothills of Black Mountain. Their faces were expressionless and their sleepwalker eyes saw only what Lord Maelstrom allowed them to see. Their mission was to drain the life force and colour from Tropal and to enslave its peoples under his command. They would all become his instruments to seek out the Tree of Spells and to bring him the one called Frog.

'Go!' he commanded. 'Go and poison your homeland. How will they stop you? They dare not harm the children, the friends, the kin who were once their own. They will gladly fall into your arms and embrace you in your misery.'

He stood high upon a rocky outcrop, a shifting, malevolent spectre, his black and blood-red-streaked robes flapped around him like the ragged tatters of wind-torn souls.

'Bring down the Canopy and destroy any foolish hope that they may cling to.'

The lost children of Tropal surged forwards like a sickly grey tide. They swept out from the barren rocks until with outstretched arms they touched the forest with their colourless poison. Grey and black replaced vibrant greens and browns. All other colours of nature's making dissolved and faded away. Trees creaked and groaned as leaves curled and withered. Ancient trunks split and cracked open, and many fell, uprooted and tangled in the spreading desolation.

Deeper and deeper into the forest, the children moved with mindless destruction. Birds, animals, all living things that could move fast enough fled; anything that could not was turned into a grey shell of its previous self.

The horde moved steadily and relentlessly onwards, never stopping, never sleeping, until their ranks stumbled out onto a wide corridor of flat ground. In the distance, the Canopy and its treetop homes towered in defiance, and standing before it in protective lines were the forest people, their faces determined and grave, a living barrier. The Guardian, saffron robes shimmering with magic, now stood as a towering figure, his shape and form somehow larger in stature.

'People of Tropal. Behold, the taken ones.' His voice echoed across the clearing and up into the Canopy. 'Do not shy away from your task today. Do not falter. Be courageous and release them from the evil and free their minds.'

The globe on his staff burned like a furnace, with a light so fierce that it could not be looked at. He spoke unheard, ancient words, and sun-bright sparks streamed up into the air to form floating, lightning-white clouds. For just a moment, the lost children of Tropal closed their eyes and hesitated, their grey bodies frozen in uncertainty. An eerie silence threw a blanket across the scene, and only those who were truly alive could hear their own heartbeats. Then the grey legion's eyelids flashed open, and a dull silver light shone out from where their eyes should have been. In unison, they stretched out their arms, and with zombie-like ignorance, they shuffled forwards.

'Courage!' shouted the Guardian. 'These are the shells of those who you once knew. You must be steadfast to release them from their torment.'

To his right, a man shouted in recognition, 'My son!' And he desperately lurched forwards from the line.

The Guardian swept out an arm and a stream of blue mist flew out to envelope the man and melt into his clothing. Instantly, he dropped to the floor, unconscious and sleeping.

'Let no one else be so foolish,' shouted the Guardian.

The lines of mindless children advanced closer and closer until the Guardian brought the base of his staff down to the ground. Above them, the bright, flashing clouds burst open with energy and rained electric sparks down onto the shuffling mass.

'Now!' commanded the Guardian.

Blowpipes were raised along the defending lines, and tainted darts flew out at the children. In their mindless task, they felt nothing as glowing embers melted into their heads and pinpricks of oblivion pierced their skin.

As their senses were drugged into darkness, grey wisps of sickly vapour escaped from their mouths, and their colourless forms regained healthy shades as their exorcised bodies crumpled to the ground.

Still they came, row upon row, and each time, sparks and blow darts made their mark, until, at the risk of being overrun, the Guardian ordered the people of the Canopy to retreat to the safety of the trees. Then, from the higher limbs, they watched as the remainder of the entranced children encircled him. He seemed to draw them to him, and they clamoured and jostled to reach his body with their outstretched arms. In desperation, they swamped over him and pulled him down beneath a mound of their clawing, flailing hands and writhing bodies, until there was nothing of him to be seen.

28.

GLACIER PASS

Frog and Mystra watched as Locrin flew off into the distance. Her parting words still echoed in their minds. 'Remember, you must cross the glacier by nightfall. You will not survive a night on the ice.' After a brief farewell, she had left them on a wide, rocky outcrop halfway up the hillside where the air was already cooler.

Now, a heavy weight descended upon their mood, and an unexplained gloom swept through their minds leaving a sense of foreboding in their hearts. They looked at each other.

'Did you feel that?' asked Mystra.

'Something's happening,' said Frog. 'Something, not good.'

'Then we'd better get a move on,' said Mystra. 'I think that it is a warning.' She gathered her leather pack and slung it over her shoulder.

Frog did the same and led the way along a narrow stone-strewn track, which led along a gully to where sheer rock walls towered high above them. As they passed into the shadows, a cold chill ran through their bones. Frog heard a sharp gasp come from behind him, and he turned to see Mystra, her head bowed and her hands grasping onto a rock for support, as if in a faint.

'What is it, Mystra? What's wrong?'

'So many voices,' she sobbed. 'I can hear them, crying out.'

He put his arm around her and helped her forwards. 'Come on, we've got to get out of here.'

Both of them felt as if a great burden was trying weigh them down and pull them back, and as they stumbled upwards, their minds filled with dark images. Ahead, Frog could just make out a shaft of sunlight through a narrow exit.

'Keep going,' he encouraged. 'Nearly there.'

With an effort, which almost sapped their strength, they pushed themselves forwards, until the clear light of day spread across Frog's face. In an instant, his head and senses cleared, as if he had broken through the surface of muddy water. Mystra felt no more like a dead weight, and he pulled her out into the sunlight. There, they lay on their backs, staring up into the clear sky.

'The lost children. He's using them against us,' said Mystra, quietly.

'I know,' said Frog. 'In my mind, I saw the Guardian surrounded by them.'

'What happened?'

'I didn't see any more,' he replied. 'Everything went dark.' He propped himself up on one elbow. 'How are you feeling now?'

She sat up, slowly. 'I've felt better.'

'We're going to have to be extra wary from now on,' he said. '*He* knows that we're coming.'

After a few minutes' rest, they set off again. The pass opened out to a landscape of rising rocks that slanted above and away from them, as if violently pushed up from the earth. They continued to travel upwards, sometimes easing their way around large, jagged boulders, sometimes scrabbling on their hands and knees up steep, small-stoned crests, until finally, they reached the top of the ridge.

A gust of ice-cold air hit them, stealing warmth like a thief, and they pulled up the fur-lined hoods of their coats closer around their heads. The scene below took their breath away. Spread out before them, a grey-white glacier carpeted a wide valley, and in the distance, Black Mountain towered in all its threatening majesty.

'It looks such a long way,' said Mystra. 'Do you think that we can make it before nightfall?'

Before Frog could answer, the ground beneath their feet rumbled and vibrated. Rocks tumbled down from high above in a crashing avalanche of destruction to fill the passageway behind them. They had no option but to continue forwards.

'Looks like our minds have been made up for us,' said Frog, as the dust settled. 'He's waiting for us. Let's not disappoint him.'

With grim determination, they started their descent to the floor of the glacier. Loose rocks and stones gave way beneath them and they slid and scraped their way down onto the freezing landscape. The glacier spread out before them, its surface a mixture of cracks, crevices and treacherous openings.

Slowly at first, they picked their way around frozen bottomless maws and over broad spans of ice.

'I sense that it is late in the day,' announced Mystra. 'And we're not even halfway.'

'Then we had better pick up the pace,' said Frog, as he stamped his feet. 'It'll also help to warm us up. If it's this cold now, I hate to think what it's like after dark!'

As they progressed, their confidence grew, almost to the point of recklessness, until Frog misjudged a leap over an icy gap. His feet landed on the frozen brink, which crumbled under his weight. He cartwheeled his arms in a desperate effort to retain his balance, but the force of gravity pulled him down, and he came to rest across the edge; his hands clawed frantically at icy chunks as he tried to prevent himself from sliding into the dark abyss, and his feet kicked out aimlessly into empty air behind him.

'Mystraaaaaa!' he yelled.

On the other side, Mystra ran in terror and threw herself at the gap; thankfully, her adrenalin gave her the much-needed boost, and she flew over Frog's flailing body to land roughly and painfully on the hard surface. Her eyes met Frog's as she scrabbled on her stomach, arms outstretched towards him. A breathless gasp escaped her lips as his head and frost-covered fingers slid out of sight.

Stunned, she stared at the space where moments ago Frog had been, and her face matched the same awful colours of the glacier. She laid there, her arms still outstretched, her mind numbed and the image of Frog's last pleading expression tattooed on her memory. The shock of losing him paralysed her.

It seemed that she had lain there for a lifetime, lost in her loneliness, until a voice invaded her despair.

'Well, are you going to help me out of here or not?'

Her senses jolted into action, and she belly-crawled to the edge. There, less than a metre below her, on a narrow ledge, Frog half hung, half perched. His gloved hands gripped around the hilt of his sword, which was firmly wedged into a crack in the wall of the crevasse.

'You're alive!' she squealed.

'Alive and freezing, and not to be too dramatic, but I can't feel my fingers, so if you don't mind...'

Mystra uncoiled a length of rope from her backpack and threw it down to Frog, who with one hand, hastily wrapped it around himself. With a joint effort, he was hauled up and he scrabbled away from the edge. Together, they lay on their backs, panting plumes of hot breath into the air.

'Well, I suppose that's one way to warm up!' he said.

She turned to him. 'Don't ever scare me like that again!' she shouted as she thumped him on the arm. The third thump turned into a hug. 'I don't know what I would have done if I'd lost you,' she whispered.

'Oh. I'm sure that you would've survived.' He grinned, as he soaked up her affection.

As a reminder that the glacier was a moving thing, the ice creaked and shifted beneath them, and they both leapt up in alarm.

'Come on,' said Frog. 'Let's get a move on. I don't want to be stuck on this thing for any longer than necessary.'

'No more taking risks,' warned Mystra. 'We have to reach the mountain before nightfall, or all will be lost.'

'Okay. Okay. I'll be careful,' he promised.

As they trudged forwards, a breeze rose up, and they could feel the cold easing its way through the fabric of their clothes and creeping into their bones. This was a dark cold that carried with it tiredness, sleep, and eventually, death.

'Look,' Frog pointed. 'We're much nearer. Not far to go now,' he encouraged.

Mystra looked up. Less than a mile in the distance, the ice gave way to the cobalt rocks that formed the base of the mountain range, in the centre of which stood Black Mountain; its great towering shape now dominated the skyline.

They worked their way through littered chunks of large ice boulders, making good progress, until another obstacle came into view that made their hearts sink as they realised what was now between them and their goal. A broad ravine far too wide for either of them to jump snaked across their path and blocked their way. Frog kicked at a lump of ice, which fell without a sound into the unfathomable darkness below.

'It will s-s-soon be d-d-dark,' said Mystra, her teeth chattering. 'We're n-n-not going to m-m-make it in time.'

'There!' Frog pointed. 'Quick, follow me.'

To their left loomed the silver-grey shape of a bridge, a natural ice structure that curved high at its centre as it spanned the crevasse. It was just wide enough to allow them to cross one at a time. Whether it would support their weight would shortly be determined.

'I'll go first,' volunteered Frog.

'No. I'm lighter than y-y-you,' said Mystra. 'When I get across, I c-c-can secure a rope and throw you the other end to tie around you.'

'Okay. Sounds like a good plan to me,' he agreed.

Mystra took off her backpack, got down on her knees and edged herself forwards, shuffling the pack before her. She strained to keep her grip as she crept up towards the highest point until, suspended halfway across, she paused.

'What's wrong?' he asked.

'It's okay. I'm just taking a rest.'

'Well, just don't look down,' warned Frog.

This, unfortunately, was not the best thing to say. If anything, Mystra was overwhelmed with the temptation, and uncontrollably she looked into the depths. A rollercoaster of dizziness swept across her senses and she froze, not from the cold, but from terror. Vertigo swept over her in a gut-churning wave. She buried her eyes in her hands and hunkered up into a ball as the wind showered her with fine particles of ice.

She crouched there, unmoving, not responding to his calls. He guessed what had happened, and silently blamed himself. *Can't keep your stupid mouth shut, can you? Right, if it's meant to be, then we'll go together,* he thought.

He knelt down, scuffled forwards, and inched his way towards her. The bridge creaked like dry wood beneath him, and a crack zigzagged crazily along the surface. Cold sweat formed on his forehead only to freeze as crystals in the now gusting wind. His head spun, and he realised that he had been holding his breath in concentration. Slowly, slowly, he moved forwards until his hands touched Mystra's feet.

'Mystra!'

No answer.

'Mystra! Listen to me. I don't know how long this bridge is going to hold out for – we have to move fast.'

No response.

'Mystra! You have to move. Now!'

Nothing.

He had heard somewhere that sometimes, people need to be shocked out of their fear, and so, he did the only thing that he could think of. He removed his gloves, and shoved his freezing cold hands under her clothing. Reluctantly, he pinched the bare skin of her legs as hard as he could.

Her head shot up with a yell. Quickly, and before she could move and send them both tipping over the edge, he gripped her ankles.

'Stay still,' he warned. 'You must do exactly as I say. Do you understand Mystra?'

There was a pause. Then… 'Frog. I'm scared.'

'So am I, but we're going to get out of this. Now listen. When I let go of your legs I want you to stretch yourself out, and I'm going to push you forwards. You should slide down the incline and all the way to the other side. Okay?'

'Okay,' came an uncertain and muffled reply.

Frog put all of his weight into pushing Mystra's body forwards, until she began to slide away from him, picking up speed as she travelled down towards the other end of the bridge. The momentum took her all the way onto the solid ice of the glacier. She rolled herself over and knelt, her body trembling with relief and from the cold as she brushed the frozen snow and ice from her.

On the centre of the bridge, Frog crouched and took off his backpack. 'Mystra,' he shouted. 'Catch.' He slowly got to his feet and swung the pack like a pendulum. As he let it go, the ground shuddered, and he struggled to keep his balance as tremors ran along the length of the bridge.

His pack landed at Mystra's feet; however, she was oblivious to it – her eyes were firmly focussed on what was happening behind Frog.

'Run!' she screamed. The word exploded from her mouth.

The far end of the bridge was crumbling in shards of broken ice, which tumbled aimlessly into the empty dark below. Frog glanced back as the disintegrating structure raced towards him as if being consumed by an invisible monster. He launched himself headfirst down the slope and prayed that there was enough force to propel him to safety. As the crest of the ice-bridge shattered, the slab of ice beneath Frog lifted at an almost vertical angle and he surged forwards along the remains of the structure ahead of him; he sped down it like a runaway train, hit the bottom curve and sailed out in mid-air to fall with a breathless thump onto the unforgiving, concrete-hard surface of the glacier.

As the remains of the bridge tumbled into the void, he stared up into Mystra's face, and with freezing tears of pain crusting in the corners of his eyes, he groaned. 'That hurt.'

Beneath them, the glacier shifted again, and great shards of ice blasted up like giant crystal spearheads pointing towards the sky. Frozen fury erupted everywhere around them, filling the air with knife-sharp icicles.

Forgetting about his pain, Frog leapt to his feet, and grabbed his backpack with one hand and Mystra's arm with the other. 'Run! Run for your life!'

They hung on to each other; hand clasped in hand as giant teeth of ice splintered around them. They sprinted, dodging this way and that, ducking and diving from chunks of shattered glacier. Their hearing was assaulted by the deafening sound of screaming, cracking ice. The wind rose to a howling fury. It whipped their clothing around them in vicious gusts. On the commands of a darker force, the glacier craved for them, and it hunted them as its prey.

His eyes closed to slits, Frog kept his focus on the looming Black Mountain ahead. 'Nearly there,' he shouted as they leapt aside to avoid a crashing frozen monolith.

Mystra tugged on his arm. 'Too late!'

Night fell as a blanket of moon-shadowed darkness.

The glacier stilled itself, and in an instant, there was nothing but the sound of the blizzard.

They held on to each other as ice crystals formed in the air around them. They could feel the frost penetrating their clothes, reaching in to freeze the blood in their hearts.

The wind whipped snow and ice around them. Their world became a blast freezer from hell.

'Mystra, we have to move.' Frog's voice came out in a frozen whisper. 'We'll die here.'

'I'm so c-c-cold,' she shivered. 'I can't feel anything, and I'm s-s-so tired. I just want to sleep.'

'No! If we fall asleep, we'll never wake up.'

He forced himself forwards. His feet would only shuffle; he had no strength left to lift his numb limbs. He gritted his teeth and called upon what little energy reserves remained. Mystra was a dead weight; he could feel her body sagging as he managed to force himself to move another step. Ice now encrusted their clothes, and they were becoming encased like frozen mummies.

Frog felt his own eyelids flutter as a cold-induced sleep shut down his senses. He hung on to her, and as their embraced bodies fell forwards into the gathering snow, the wind howled in triumph.

29.

THE IMMORTALS

The surge of mindless children had grown into a pillar of writhing bodies, beneath which the Guardian had been overwhelmed. In the trees of the Canopy, the forest people watched with helpless horror. When every shuffling, possessed child had been drawn to the struggling mass, a dull thud resonated through the ground; those in the trees felt, rather than heard, the shockwave.

Like feathers on a breeze, their limp figures tumbled to the ground, falling away to reveal the Guardian who still stood, upright and untouched. The children lay scattered and strewn around him, their bodies now bathed in healthy colours.

He stretched out his arms. 'People of the Canopy. Come and reclaim your sons and daughters, they are again as one with the forest.'

Children all around him began to open their eyes and sit up as if waking from a deep sleep, and as families were reunited in happy and tearful embraces, none noticed the Guardian step away to the edge of the forest and set his gaze to the north, in the direction of Glacier Pass and Black Mountain.

In the ancient history of Tropal, when the forest was young and vulnerable, there lived a race of foresters who devoted themselves to the protection of the trees. Born of a union of elves and men, they dedicated their lives to the well-being and growth of the woodland. Many times, they defended the forest from Slipstream travellers and marauders who thought nothing of taking an axe to the trees.

In such a time, a race of plunderers invaded Tropal, and in a great battle, the foresters paid the ultimate sacrifice – they used their own life force to destroy their enemies and save the forest. A Guardian was appointed to Tropal, and as a reward for their martyrdom and bravery, he gave the forester's souls immortality. They had but one chance to unite with any living host, but should they choose to remain in that form, their immortality would cease. Despite their powers to heal others, they themselves would eventually die, unless they returned to the eternal confines of the Cradle.

The Guardian stood motionless, his eyes closed, his mind focussed on a world of ice and snow, and he gently tapped the base of his staff into the earth. Two burning globes floated down from the Cradle, and hovered in front of him

'Quickly, to the north; I sense the Chosen one

and his companion are in danger.' He spread his arms wide and summoned an urgent breeze to carry the golden orbs away far above the trees. 'For all our sakes, let them not be too late,' he prayed.

With that concern in his mind, he turned his devotion to his people and the task ahead.

30.

THE LAIR OF THE SNOW BEAR

Hot breath invaded Mystra's semi-conscious thoughts. Her face was warm, and the warmth penetrated her senses. She opened her eyes to see a great, black snout and two slate-grey pupils staring into her face.

Wake. The voice rumbled in her head as if it was distant thunder. *Wake! Your destiny is not to die here. Get up and climb onto my back.* A large paw scooped her up and she found herself pressed against a wall of warm, white fur. *Climb onto my back and hold on.*

'Frog!' she cried. 'Where's Frog?' She turned her head and the howling gale threw piercing granules of snow into her eyes.

Do not concern yourself; my brother carries him. Now, climb onto my back.

'Are you friend or foe?' she asked.

I am a formidable foe, and if you do not climb onto my back, I may well decide to be less friendly. Now hurry!

Reluctantly, Mystra hauled herself up into the

thick, white fur, which folded its warmth around her. She reached out for Frog with her mind. *Frog! Frog! Speak to me. Where are you?*

I'm on the back of a massive white bear. Where are you? he replied.

Before she could answer, the growling voice of another bear interrupted her thoughts. *Silence, both of you, or I will tear your heads from your bodies!*

The menace in the bear's voice was enough to convince both Frog and Mystra to be quiet, although whether they had been captured or rescued still remained a question to be answered.

Even though a blizzard howled and swept around them, deep within the bear's fur, their bodies regained valuable core heat. The lumbering motion of the bear's progress, and the warmth that now soaked into every corner of their beings had a hypnotic effect on them, and they willingly embraced the comfort and fell into a dreamless sleep.

It was a deep rhythmic breathing and the dull thump of a heartbeat that awoke Frog. A silver beam of moonlight streamed through the cave's entrance, and he observed the enormous bulk of a Snow Bear spread out opposite him, with Mystra asleep between its great black, padded paws. His own position was not dissimilar; a large fur-clad arm rested across his body. Whether this was an embrace of protection or one of restraint continued to be unknown.

'Mystra!' he whispered. 'Mystra!'

She stirred gently.

Mystra, wake up! he called with his mind, and her eyes opened to meet his.

Warily, they slipped away from the bears' embraces, and slowly and silently crept from the mouth of the cave, to make their way out into the dark volcanic landscape that made up the foothills of Black Mountain. The silver disc of a moon hovered overhead and reflected dully on the still and silent glacier, which brooded far below. They were now quite a distance up, and both of them were surprised at how far they had been carried. The air, although cold, was no longer freezing.

'It's nearly daybreak,' said Mystra.

'Then we'd best get moving before those bears wake up,' suggested Frog.

'I'm not sure that they would have harmed us,' said Mystra.

'I think that it's better for us not to wait and find out,' replied Frog.

They clambered up onto a wide ridge, where a sheer cliff face towered up on one side. To their right, shale and crumbled rock slanted down for many metres into a ravine. Ahead, a tall pillar of dark rock leaned almost lazily against the cliff to create a natural arch, under which was the only pathway.

'This way,' said Frog.

As they neared the arch, a dark shadow emerged

to block their way. A giant, black mountain bear reared up in front of them. Its bulk was twice the size of the Snow Bears, and with an almighty roar, it lunged forwards, to swipe an enormous clawed paw at them. Frog fell to one side and scrabbled backwards like a retreating crab, while Mystra lost her footing and fell onto the gravel slope, which started to shift beneath her weight. She reached out with one arm and grabbed onto a protruding rock, aimlessly kicking out with her feet. She struggled to climb back up, but the ground beneath her legs began to avalanche away.

Frog regained his feet, drew his sword and valiantly jabbed at the beast. It growled again and responded with another clawed swipe; this time it knocked the sword from Frog's grasp and sent it clattering along the track. As Frog stumbled backwards into a small gap in the rocks, the bear shook its head, and long sinews of drool snaked from its mouth. It roared in triumph as it realised that there was no escape for Frog, and it moved forwards to tear him apart.

A fist-sized lump of rock bounced almost comically off the bear's head.

'Pick on someone your own size!' shouted Mystra, who had managed to find purchase on the protruding boulder and heave herself up to the edge. She threw another large rock, which again connected with the bear's head, this time, right between its eyes. This seemed to cause it some irritation, but only such as that of a bothersome fly, and for a second, it took its attention away from Frog, who seized the moment to leap for his sword. The bear, however, had other ideas, and it brought a clawed fist backwards to hit Frog with the force of a tree trunk. It caught him across his body and sent him flailing to land unconscious against the cliff. Satisfied that Frog was not moving, the animal turned to Mystra, and with an easy bound, it reached out. She turned her back in an act of futile defence, and a claw snagged her backpack.

Hooked onto its great paw, she was raised up and dangled like a struggling marionette. With a grunt, it threw her sideways and she landed beside Frog's motionless figure. In desperation, she shielded Frog's body as the bear loomed over them; it gave a low, throaty growl almost as if it was savouring her fear, before it moved in for the kill.

A white ball of fury slammed into the bear, taking it sideways, driving it along the track. A second hulk of white fur hurtled past, and Mystra gasped as she watched the two Snow Bears assault the beast. Claws and fangs clashed. Deep red blood seeped through white fur, and the noise of pain and aggression was terrifying to her ears.

The gigantic creature somehow managed to raise itself up onto its hind legs as one Snow Bear clung on to its broad back, whilst the other hung on with its teeth gripped firmly around a black furred leg in an attempt to pull the beast off balance. The black bear lashed out and a set of claws scraped along the rock wall to send out a shower of tiny sparks.

Frog stirred beside Mystra, and his eyes flicked opened to the scene. He shook his head to clear his senses.

'Are you alright?' he said.

'I'm okay, just a bit shaken,' said Mystra. 'What about you?'

Frog eased himself up. 'I think that I'll live,' he said with a grimace. His fingers gingerly felt a bloodied lump on the back of his head.

An ear-piercing roar filled the air, and they both looked on in horror as the black bear summoned up its enormous strength to swipe the Snow Bear from its leg, and send it flailing over the side of the track and down into the ravine on a landslide of shale. Then it swung its great bulk around and crushed the other bear between itself and the cliff. The Snow Bear lost its grip and slid to the floor, its senses stunned. The great beast roared in triumph. Although blood ran freely from its claw-raked face and body, it moved confidently in to slaughter the stunned Snow Bear. It stretched its jaws wide open and exposed its yellow fanged teeth ready to tear at the dazed bear's throat as it leant forwards for the kill.

In an instant, everything changed. Its expression froze as shock masked its face, and its eyes widened with a look of surprise. Paralysed in death, it fell forwards and hit the ground with a last living gasp of expelled air.

The fallen Snow Bear opened its eyes to see Frog astride the dead beast's back, his sword buried up to its hilt in the black fur of its shoulder blades.

'Just like most bullies,' said Frog. 'In the end, the bigger they are, the harder they fall.'

In that moment, daylight blinked away the night and the injuries to the Snow Bear looked horrific to Mystra's and Frog's eyes.

'I'm so sorry that we snuck away,' she said. 'But we didn't know what you were going to do with us.'

The Snow Bear's voice came into her head. *I learnt long ago that in troubled times trust is hardest earned and quickly sacrificed. You only did what you thought was necessary.*

Frog moved to the edge of the ravine and looked down. In the distance, the other Snow Bear, its coat now a dirty grey, was making its way to the pathway that led up to the cave.

'Your brother looks as though he is alright, and he's on his way back up.'

Give me some room. I need to stand. The Snow Bear raised himself on all fours and shook his fur the length of his body.

'You look terribly hurt,' said Mystra, as she studied with growing concern, the bloodied, matted streaks in the bear's coat, and the angry red claw marks along its muzzle.

It is of no significance. It will heal. Let us return to the cave. Who knows what other dangers lurk amongst these rocks.

Frog retrieved his sword and climbed down. 'I'm sorry that I doubted you, but I have spent enough time in the Dimensions to be wary of strangers. Human or animal.'

What makes you think that we are just animals, young Frog? I thought that you were taught long ago that things are not always as they seem.

With a sideways glance, the Snow Bear shuffled past, leaving Frog with an expression of surprise on his face.

Well, are you coming? the bear teased.

Once inside the cave, Mystra turned to the bear. 'Here,' she said. 'Let me.' She soaked one of her gloves with water from her canteen, and gently dabbed the bear's snout to wipe away the crusted blood. After a few moments, she paused. 'I don't believe it!'

'What?' said Frog.

'Look, there's nothing. Not a mark!'

The other Snow Bear ambled into the cave, grunted irritably, sat on his haunches in a corner, and proceeded to lick at his already healing wounds.

Forgive my brother; he does not gladly take to the inconveniences of a living body, and craves to return to the Cradle.

Mystra stared, her eyes like saucers. 'Are you… Immortals?'

We have the power to heal whilst we inhabit these life forms, but if they were to die, then so would we, especially this far from the Cradle. It is only there that we are truly Immortals. The Guardian sensed your plight, and released us to your aid.

Frog managed to pull his senses together. 'I truly thank you for saving our lives.'

And I thank you for saving my existence and this bear's life. It would not have recovered from such a mortal injury, and I also would have perished.

'What are we to do now?' asked Frog.

We are to escort you to Black Mountain Gate. There, you shall journey onwards and we must return to the Cradle, and leave these bears to their unknowing lives. The Snow Bear turned to Frog. *Before we proceed, I have two gifts. Hold out your damaged hand.*

Frog held up the hand with the stub of a little finger on it, which had been severed by the vile wolf, Fangmaster, during his first adventures in the Dimension of Castellion. The Snow Bear extended a long, pink tongue and licked at the hand. Frog let out a short, nervous laugh at the wet, fleshy sensation. He caught his breath as the digit began to rejuvenate; skin and bone painlessly stretched and grew into a complete finger.

He held it up to his face, and flexed it. 'It's like new!' He smiled.

Here, this is also for you. The bear held out its huge paw. In the centre of the jet-black pad sat a large, sharp-pointed, yellow claw.

'What's this?' asked Frog.

It is from the beast; I found it beside the brute after you had slain it. It is your battle trophy, a symbol of your bravery. Carry it with honour.

Frog took the claw; it nearly filled the palm of his hand. 'I'm not sure what I would do with such a thing.'

'I know,' said Mystra. She took it and turned to her backpack, where she pulled out a leather thong, which she secured it around the claw. 'You must wear it,' she said as she placed the thong over his head and around his neck.

The claw settled in the centre of his chest.

Let it be a warning to all of what a brave and formidable foe you are. The Snow Bear declared.

'I'm not sure about that,' said Frog, as he felt his face redden.

It was at that moment, Frog learnt that sarcasm comes in many forms – the voice of the other bear entered his head. *We have fulfilled the Guardian's command, and this is all very touching, but I would like to return to the haven of the Cradle. Can we go now?*

31.

MAELSTROM'S RAGE

Lord Maelstrom stormed through the subterranean corridors; he lashed out at anything that moved. In a mindless rage, green jagged power streaked from his hands to wantonly maim and destroy even the vilest creatures of his creation.

'Have I not the powers to control the elements? Do I not command my will to be done?' Another furious burst of destructive power streaked out. 'I will destroy that meddling Guardian; I will ring the life force from his soul. I *shall* have the power of the Tree of Spells!'

He made his way out of the tunnels and onto a ledge, which towered high above the floor of a huge hewn-out underground citadel. His cloak rippled with the faces of a thousand screaming souls, and he looked down to the floor, which writhed with all manner of creatures, some of nature's making and some that should not exist in any world, all of which had been conjured up in the name of evil.

The stench of brimstone and toxic gases filled the air. Molten pools spewed out lava that bubbled with long-lost elements from deep within the earth. Furnaces forged vicious weapons whilst others disgorged more half-living things to swell the ranks of Lord Maelstrom's unearthly army. He addressed them from his balcony. His voice boomed and echoed with hate and malice.

'More! I must have more. This army shall sweep across Tropal like a tide of death, and then on to Terrae, the boy's Dimension. I will take his world. I will have my war. I will rule the Dimensions.'

He called out to some of the horrors of his creation, to the leather-winged creatures that resembled prehistoric pterodactyls. He also summoned other terrors; giant, eyeless mole-like creatures, and they scrabbled out from hiding places in the dark shadows and recesses. As monstrous as they were, even they cowered at his gaze.

'Go!' he commanded. 'Search out the secret places. Find me the Tree of Spells!'

32.

BLACK MOUNTAIN GATE

Escorted by the Snow Bears, their journey up through the black, lava-strewn slopes to the base of Black Mountain was thankfully uneventful.

One of the Snow Bears turned to Frog and Mystra. *The gate is not far ahead. This is where we leave; we must return our hosts to their cave and then take flight back to the Cradle.*

'Will the bears remember nothing?' asked Mystra.

A trace recollection, like the whispers of a distant dream. That is all.

With the back of her hand, she gave the animal a soft stroke down along its face and broad muzzle, and then, before it could move, she reached up and hugged the other bear around its neck.

Quietly, in the back of her mind, the Immortal within the bear spoke only to her.

You have the heart and courage of the forest. Come seek me out when you next return to the Cradle, and I will share my knowledge with you.

As they watched the Snow Bears amble into the shadows, a burden returned to fall upon their shoulders. Above them, covering the mountain's summit, a dark cloud swirled menacingly like a whirlpool in the sky. Reflections of red and orange flickered and shifted through its shape, and it cast a dark shadow over the landscape.

'I sense that he doesn't know we are this close,' said Frog, as he looked around guardedly. 'I think something is shielding us from his view, but I still have a feeling we are being watched by someone, or something else.'

Dark eyes did indeed observe them from high above as their owner waited patiently for the right moment to act.

They found a flight of cracked stone steps that led upwards to a rough-hewn archway, and they continued their climb,

Frog drew his sword and placed a finger to his lips. Quietly, they ascended, until they pressed their backs against the rock on either side of the arch. Frog reached down and picked up a small stone, which he tossed through the archway. They held their breath as they heard it clatter along the ground. Apart from a soft rumble, which seemed to resonate up from beneath their feet, there was no other sound.

'Let's take a chance,' suggested Frog, in a low voice.

Stealthily, they crept forwards, through the arch and onto a small plateau, to stand face to face with Black Mountain Gate.

The gate itself consisted of two identical, pitch-black wooden doors set side by side into the face of the mountain. Iron hinges held the doors fixed to the rock, and in the centre of each door was a large iron ring.

Frog took the folded leather from his pouch, and handed the crystal to Mystra.

'I think that we have to look at the doors through the crystal,' suggested Mystra. She brought it up to her eyes, and turned it around between her fingers.

'Well?' asked Frog, as she lowered it.

She wrinkled her nose. 'Nothing. Just lots of rocks.'

'We definitely need the moon, then. How long before nightfall?'

She tilted her head skywards. 'Soon.'

She was right. It wasn't long before the sky turned to a velvet black, and the silver orb of the moon cast its ghostly light across the side of the mountain.

Mystra raised the crystal to her eye once more. This time, the facets in it merged to form two clear windows, through which the doors took their shapes. One appeared unchanged, but the other was now intricately carved with ornate mystical runes and emblems.

'There!' she exclaimed, excitedly. 'The one on the right. It's the one on the right! Look.'

She handed the crystal to Frog. 'Come on, quick.' She hurried forwards. 'Let's go.'

Frog looked through the crystal as Mystra placed her hands on the iron ring to push the door open.

'No! Stop!' shouted Frog. 'Don't open it!'

Too late. The door did not open. Instead, it dissolved enough for Mystra to melt into it. Her body folded through its surface a supple as playdough, and Frog stood helpless, as he saw her puzzled and confused face dissolve. She was gone!

Frog threw himself at the door, which was now solid and unyielding.

He hammered at it savagely with his fists.

'Mystra! Mystra! Mystraaaaaa!'

For a while, he leant against the door, breathless and panting with disbelief, until he resigned to what he really knew. He slid to the floor, legs outstretched, his back against the hard wood, and he balled up his hands against his eyes as they filled with tears of sadness and anger.

Desperately, he reached out with his mind. *Mystra? Mystra? Where are you?* He conjured up visions of her smiling face. Again, he called out aloud to her. 'Mystra!' Nothing. His head pounded in a mental effort to connect with her, until, emotionally exhausted, he accepted the reality that she was gone – dragged into oblivion.

He wasn't sure how long it was that he sat there in the overbearing silence, numb and hollow with loss. His thoughts moved from sadness to anger, and then to blame. He blamed himself for not stopping her. He blamed her for acting so recklessly. He blamed the clue for tricking her. Finally, the blame turned back into anger.

'I give up!' he shouted. 'How many more friends must I lose?'

Her voice came into his head. *You must go on, for all our sakes.*

'Mystra?'

It was only a faded echo. A ghost of her memory. It didn't help, but he knew that she was right.

He sniffed and drew his arm across his face. 'Okay. For you, Mystra. I'll do it for you,' he said.

He opened the clue and studied it once more, and then he got to his feet and looked through the crystal again. Both doors appeared as before. He read the clue once more. He studied the words and ran them through his mind.

By the light of the moon. At Black Mountain's Gate. My windows shall reveal two paths. One to what you seek. The other to oblivion. Which one to take shall be plain to see.

It was that simple. The plain and undecorated door led the way. In her haste, Mystra had taken the path to oblivion, and in his heart, he knew that he had indeed lost another dear friend.

The rattling cascade of falling rocks disturbed his despair, and he looked up to see a monstrous shadow perched on a precipice overhead. Its fire-red eyes glared down at him. With a menacing flourish, two great leathery wings extended from the creature's back. This was no dragon.

His survival instinct kicked in, and without a second thought, he grabbed the iron handle of the plain door. An unseen force pulled him into its now sponge-like surface, and he slipped through as though he were the substance of a ghost.

He found himself in a long tunnel of black, glistening rock, illuminated by flaming torches. He turned around to face the door and tentatively pressed his hands to it. The grained wood was unyielding and solid. Again, there was no going back.

He put the clue and the crystal into his pouch, drew his sword, and took the next determined and heavy-hearted steps of his journey into the unknown.

The tunnel descended in a straight line. He passed the rows of torches with monotonous repetition, and at times, he felt as though he were on a treadmill. Slowly, the atmosphere changed; the walls ceased to run with moisture and the cool air was replaced with a stifling heat, to the point that he had to discard his thick layers of clothing.

Now, he stood in the loose-fitting garments

of the forest people; the sweat on his bare arms glistened in the flickering light of the torches.

His sword was in its scabbard, and secured around his waist on his belt along with his pouch and water bottle. Around his neck hung the unseen talisman on its silver chain, along with the bear's claw fixed to its leather thong.

With renewed determination, he journeyed down a path that could only lead him into the depths of the mountain. Eventually, he came to a point when all that he could see ahead was darkness, the torches came to an end and the tunnel reached a dead end against a wall of solid rock.

'What now?' His voice resonated around him.

He ran his hands over the sharp ridges and lumps of the rock as he looked for a hidden lever or a switch, but there was none. He examined the shadowed walls on either side, but to no avail. Lastly, he crouched down on the solid floor and brushed away sand and grit in the hope of discovering a hidden trapdoor. Still nothing.

He exhaled frustration. 'What's the point?' he shouted, and his words echoed back up the tunnel, as if mocking him. He leaned back against the wall and tilted his head up to stretch the stiff muscles of his neck. His eyes fell on a dark shadow above him. He blinked.

'Of course, you idiot!'

He stood up and stepped back from the wall. He

studied it, and his searching eyes began to make out a pattern of shallow foot and handholds cut into the rock. He retrieved the nearest torch from its iron wall bracket and held it up. About ten metres above him he could just make out the curve of a ledge.

He gathered two more torches and placed them on the floor to illuminate the shaft, and then he began his climb. He had no difficulty in hauling himself onto the rock platform; it was there that he was confronted with a metre square wooden hatchway. There didn't appear to be a handle, so he gave it a shove with his shoulder. The wood creaked and dust escaped from its edges, but it remained firm.

Okay, he thought. *Time for some brute force!*

He rolled onto his back, drew his knees up, and kicked out with both feet. The wood splintered apart and fell inwards; it was then that the heat hit him with the ferocity of a furnace. A red glare of light spilled over him and the stench of sulphuric smoke filled his lungs. Coughing uncontrollably, he turned his back against the heat and reached for his water bottle. Quickly, he filled his mouth with the warm, but welcome liquid, and then he tore a strip of material from his tunic, soaked it in water and secured it around his face as a protective mask.

Slowly, he crawled through the opening and stared in awe at the cauldron of stewing red lava far below. He was at the heart of Black Mountain!

Sweat ran into his eyes, and although this made them sting, at least it stopped them from drying out in the intense heat. He blinked at his surroundings; the chamber was immense. To his left, cut into the rock, a narrow walkway circled around and he could just make out an opening, a doorway, on the other side. It rippled in the heat, like a mirage.

'This had better not be a wild goose chase,' he complained, as he eased himself out and along the ledge, which now seemed far too narrow for his liking. Foolishly, he glanced down and started to feel the first twinges of vertigo.

Slowly, he eased along sideways and pressed his back against the wall, desperately trying to keep himself as far away from the edge as possible. Even so, it gave his feet only centimetres of room to spare. He spread his arms wide, using his fingers to constantly feel for precious purchase, but the wall was unnaturally smooth. Should he slip, there would be little hope of survival.

His mouth and throat was invaded by a taste similar to that produced by a chemistry experiment gone wrong. He tried not to swallow. All that he could do was lick at the salty sweat that ran across his lips.

He forced himself to stare ahead, and not to be distracted by the bellowing, hissing heat of spewing magma below.

'Don't look down. Don't look down. Don't look down,' he chanted to himself.

He was no more than a couple of metres from the exit, when the cavern rumbled. The very walls seemed to stretch and flex. Great chunks of rock fell from above and splashed into the restless lava below, to be consumed by fiery flares. His heart leapt up into his mouth as he lost his footing and fell onto one knee, with one leg dangling over the edge. Desperately, he twisted himself as flat as he could against the wall as more tremors shook the chamber. A great bulbous mass of lava erupted, and fell back into the boiling red soup of liquid and flame. The furnace of heat reached out and singed his eyebrows, and he squeezed his eyes shut as the skin on his face blistered and tightened as if it would split open. He cried out in pain.

As the vibrations subsided, he found that he did not have enough room to manoeuvre himself back up to a standing position. If he tried, his own weight would topple him into the inferno. Steeling himself, he resigned to shuffle awkwardly along to the exit, which now seemed so much further away.

Whilst he had journeyed deeper into the mountain, he was unaware that a poison tainted his every breath. Black Mountain was indeed toxic and harmful to the strength of the soul. Now, at its heart, it sapped away his confidence and weakened his determination, and as he struggled on the ledge, it engulfed his senses in its malicious misery. The weight of losing Mystra hit him like a dark, black cloud, and a feeling of despair smothered him. What was the point? He had lost yet another friend. All that his adventures had given him were sadness and fear. He couldn't go on anymore. The effort was too much. Just to let go and fall would be a quick and final release. He felt his hands relaxing their grip on the ledge, and he prepared to let himself tumble into the furnace.

Frog? Frog? Where are you? His mother's voice rippled through his mind with the soft caress of a cool breeze. The image of her caring face took shape in front of him – her kind blue eyes and the warm smile that he knew so well.

'Mum?' he spoke out loud.

Frog. You mustn't give in. Don't let him win. You can do this. You can survive.

'But I'm so tired, Mum,' he said.

You are stronger than you think.

'But it's so hard. I want to come home.'

Soon. Soon you will be home, but you must get the Tree of Spells. Can you do that – for me?

'I'll do anything for you.'

Good. I believe in you. I love you. Remember, YOU ARE THE CHOSEN ONE!

Her image faded, and in those moments, he closed his mind and called on every drop of strength and willpower that he still possessed. In the following seconds, he would either survive or he would fall.

Afterwards, he couldn't remember how he managed to get off the ledge. All he could recall was rolling into a cool tunnel and lying on his back; his mind and body spent and exhausted. Scorched and blistered, agony hesitated for a moment, ready to assault him without mercy. The last scattered thoughts that drifted across his mind were – *She called me Frog! She spoke about the Tree of Spells! She said that I was the Chosen one! How does she know about that?*

33.

BEFORE THE STORM

High in the Cradle, the Guardian stood amongst hundreds of small globes, which now floated around him as if they were performing a gentle aerial ballet. The orange mist within them swirled and flickered like surreal miniature snowstorms.

'Immortals!' the Guardian spoke. 'Tropal and its forests are threatened by the evil of the Dark Lord. Should we fall, we shall all die or become instruments of his foul army. This day I call upon you to sacrifice your immortality and to come to the aid of the Dimensions. Take whatever living forms shall willingly give themselves up to your keeping, and shield them with your ancient armour.

'The Chosen one seeks to save the Tree of Spells, but whether he should succeed or not, we shall be confronted by the Dark Lord's minions on the open plains of the Flatlands in two days' time. It is there that the battle for this Dimension shall be won or lost. I summon every living thing of good nature from the air and earth of Tropal to assemble in its defence, and so I release you also to play your part in our destiny.'

The globes twisted and spiralled around him. He stood at the centre of a whirlwind of pulsating, flashing energy, which rose into a column and stretched up into the sky. With the sound of a rushing tide, the globes scattered into the depths of the forest as if they were pollen on an urgent wind.

Later, following the Afterglow, the Guardian addressed the Council of Tropal. Their youthful faces, behind which they held knowledge well beyond their years, all focussed on his every word.

'None thought that this day would come, when the tranquillity of Tropal and its survival could be threatened in such a way. In other worlds, in other Dimensions, you would be regarded as children, too young for a burden and a task such as this, but we know that you possess the resolve and courage of your hidden years. There is a great power within the forests and it will answer the call to strengthen your people. Now, join the circle; the time has come to unite as one.'

The Council formed around him, arms outstretched with their hands on each other's shoulders. Silently, the Guardian mouthed a passage of ancient words, which had not been uttered since the beginning of time, and as he spoke them, the yew leaf circlets on the Council's heads began to radiate a soft green light, which pulsated slowly, and formed into small vaporous clouds. As the Council picked up the chant and repeated it with the Guardian, the green mist swelled and poured out like a billowing, rolling river. It tumbled over the sides of the Cradle, down along the walkways, and out into the forest and beyond, where it washed over every living thing in its path.

The Guardian raised his staff and the chant stopped, and the last wispy tendrils of vapour slipped into the forest to spread its healing magic.

'Go! Prepare all who have the strength to pull a bow, wield a sword, and fight against the dark army that would enslave us.'

★★★

During the next two days, a multitude of living things began to emerge from the forests of Tropal, to assemble on the Flatlands. Herds of emerald green unicorns with formidable, curled horns appeared from secret glades. Forest elephants came with their menacing ivory tusks. Great silver-backed gorillas travelled from the high grounds. Sabre-toothed pumas descended from the mountain ranges and congregated with their rainforest cousins; the panthers, leopards and jaguars. All were united against the evil that threatened their Dimension.

On the morning of the second day, the people of Tropal began to assemble, now transformed into a warrior nation. Green banners and ensigns with images of gold trees emblazoned upon them were hoisted high and unfurled by the Council, who to any outsider, would appear to be too young to bear arms, too innocent for conflict. Nevertheless, their appearance was deceptive; behind their youthful exterior, they were very much men and women of great maturity and strength.

The army of Tropal carried a great variety of armour and weapons: blowpipes, which they could use with great skill and accuracy, along with bows, swords and shields from a long-forgotten race – an armoury that had lain hidden in secret places, but was now released by the Guardian into the hands of the forest people.

They came in their thousands, proud and defiant, all joined by a common cause. Never before had so many different life forms gathered together in unity. The throng reached out in rows hundreds deep. Under a grey and gloomy sky, they waited. The great orb of the sun was now obscured from sight by Lord Maelstrom's evil magic.

★★★

In the Valley of the Horsemen, Jorge sat at a campfire, warming his hands against the chill of early morning.

Dagar stood talking with another Horseman when, their conversation was interrupted as the ground violently shuddered.

'Is it an earthquake?' asked Jorge. He tried to get to his feet, only to be thrown off balance and fall to his knees.

'The ground has never had cause to move here in the Valley,' replied Dagar. 'Something is happening outside.'

The tremor stopped as abruptly as it had started, the sound replaced by the thunder of approaching hooves that heralded the arrival of two more Horsemen.

'Dagar! The Valley entrance has been cleared,' announced one of them. 'The rock has fallen away and the corridor is open. At last we can be free.'

'Wait here,' Dagar instructed Jorge.

Jorge got to his feet and blocked Dagar's way. 'No! I'm part of this, and I'm staying with you no matter what happens.'

Dagar glowered down, and he stamped a hoof, clearly meaning to intimidate Jorge.

Jorge stood his ground. Deep inside, he also did not trust the Horseman. For a few seconds he locked eyes with Dagar.

'You are either fearless or foolish,' said Dagar. 'Get on my back, for soon we shall find out which.'

By the time that Jorge and Dagar arrived, numerous Horsemen filled the scene around the newly cleared passageway, and Dagar had to push himself through the throng, bellowing in his deep voice. 'Make way! Make way!'

Where the rock face had sealed over Frog, Mystra and Jorge's entrance, there was now a wide, towering ravine; its exit at the other end was clearly visible.

Locrin approached. 'The time of our release has come,' she said to Dagar. 'Let us ride out and claim our freedom.'

'Ride out to what?' questioned Dagar. 'Perhaps we should not be in such a hurry to join a battle that is not ours. What use is freedom to the dead? We should wait and see what unfolds.' There were some murmurs of agreement around him.

'But you promised!' pleaded Jorge as he slid from Dagar's back.

'I promised nothing!' Dagar bellowed. 'For whatever reason, the way out is now clear. It could be that the Guardian and the people of Tropal have been defeated; if so, then there is no need for us to sacrifice ourselves to a lost cause. We have suffered enough, locked away in exile. All I taste is bitterness.'

'What if they haven't been defeated?' argued Jorge. 'What if they are still fighting, and their survival and the future of Tropal depends on you and your people?'

Dagar looked stubbornly at Jorge. 'Give me one good reason why I should trust a Guardian and lead my people into battle?'

Jorge walked to the entrance of the ravine. 'I can think of a hundred reasons, but it should not need me to remind you of them. Everybody makes mistakes, whether it's through selfishness or ignorance. Sometimes there is a price to pay, but as long as they learn from it, they will become stronger and wiser. If, after all this time, you've learnt nothing, then I truly pity you. All I know is that I have friends and family out there, fighting for good, fighting for each other and survival, and with or without you, I'm not going to let them down.'

'If you go, you die!' shouted Dagar.

'I don't care whether that's a threat or a warning. At least I'll die for those that I love, and I'll die with honour, and for the good. Will you be able to say the same?'

He turned his back and made his way down the long gorge. Fear had left his heart, and the battle for Tropal beckoned him.

34.

THE FINAL CLUE

Frog stirred, half awake. A combination of the fierce throbbing that hammered against the inside of his skull and the pain from his dry, parched throat and blistered lips, brought his mind back from the sweet abyss of deep sleep. He prised his eyelids open, and even though the tunnel was lit with only the red reflection of the mountain's furnace, his eyes hurt as if he were staring into the face of a summer's sun. He let out a breathless groan as he rolled to one side, and every part of his body complained with the assault of sharp pains and spasms.

He had never endured such agony in his life, and he felt broken, physically and mentally. He couldn't remember where he was or what he was supposed to be doing. He couldn't even remember *who* he was!

In a waking fever, bizarre visions paraded in front of him: spiders morphed into dragons, and red eye patches floated in gossamer bubbles. A faceless man stood under an apple tree, and called out his name, with a soundless voice. A red-haired woman transformed herself into a bushy-tailed fox, which then burst into flames.

His mind raced with a myriad of voices calling out to him in strange languages. Everything began to spiral and echo, each figure melting and blending into one another as the voices merged into an ear-splitting, discordant scream. Madness reached out to wipe clean what was left of his memory – to empty the remainder of his sanity. There was the sound of a door being violently slammed. Then, there was nothing but blackness and silence.

In that dark and quiet place, there appeared a small flicker of white light, a tiny flame, which flourished into the shape of a woman. She was smiling. Closer and closer, she came, and he thought that he knew her from somewhere; maybe from another dream? She reached out her hand and placed her fingers on his lips, tenderly as though she were feeding him something, something comforting and sweet. He swallowed soft, warming nectar, and in gratitude, he went to thank her, but she drifted away like the white delicate seed of a dandelion, blown by a soft breeze.

Pain. Fear. Despair. Everything foul and tormenting fell away from him as dust scattered by the wind. When he awoke fully, he felt renewed, cleansed and alive. He was sitting up, his back against the wall of the tunnel, which was still aglow with the red light of the mountain's furnace.

Tentatively, he touched his face. His skin felt soft and supple, and his eyebrows and hair were undamaged. The remains of something shifted under his tongue and he eased it out onto his lips to gently gather it between his finger and thumb. He studied the tealeaf-sized object; even in the red light, it gave off a green and silver sheen.

In his feverish state, a sixth sense must have reminded him of the healing leaves in his pouch, and somehow he had managed to place one or two in his mouth to chew on. They had worked their magic. Now, his mind was alert and clear, and there was no evidence of his injuries or wounds.

At that moment, Black Mountain seemed to give a low rumble of disapproval.

'Time to go, I think,' he responded.

Half an hour later, where the tunnel reached an intersection with five other passageways, he stood before a small alcove in which there was a simple shrine where two yellow candles burned brightly. Carved into the stone shelf of the shrine and between the candles were two images – the shapes of a small figurine and a key.

He opened his pouch and retrieved the two objects. One after the other, he placed them in the carved outlines. They fitted perfectly.

As he watched, the objects simply dissolved

into the stone. The candles flared, and the flames flickered erratically to dance shadows around the passageway walls; wax droplets flowed hurriedly down from the candles to form a new shape on the shelf, that of a small scroll.

The flames subsided, and resumed their gentle dancing, and the wax scroll hardened like a sculpture.

'Next clue, I guess,' said Frog, and he picked up the smooth, still warm object.

In the flickering light, he turned it over in his hands, and as he did so, the wax crumbled away to reveal a rolled piece of parchment. He opened it out and read its message.

THE COMPASS SHALL BRING YOU TO ME.
MY WARRIORS STAND GUARD
UNTIL YOU UNLOCK THEIR SECRET.
ONLY THEN SHALL WE MEET.

Below the writing, and drawn in detail with black ink, a circle of six grotesque faces stared back.

'They look like gargoyles,' he considered. 'Well, whatever they are, it looks as though they're the last clue,' he said, hopefully.

He brought out the compass and the needle on its face reappeared. It spun erratically as if seeking out a place, until finally, it settled to point towards an unlit passageway to the far right of him.

'I guess that I'll be needing one of these then,' he said, as he took one of the candles. 'Just don't go out on me!' he warned it.

As he stepped forwards into the tunnel, its featureless void seemed to welcome him in pursuit of his elusive goal.

He seemed to wander for hours through endless passageways, some that ran downwards, and then upwards, turning him this way and that, until he was finally rewarded – with yet another dead end!

This time however, the barrier before him was not another bleak wall of rock.

35.

The Tree

Carved into the wall were twelve gargoyle-like faces, all of them angry or sad in appearance and all laid out in a square grid pattern. The flickering candle created shadows, which passed across the faces, causing their expressions to change and alter, as if they were alive.

He fumbled in his pouch for the parchment with the drawings on it. Carefully, he studied them, and then he looked back at the ones in the wall. Six of them matched each other, but only for a second before the shifting shadows changed their appearance and distorted them, as if they moved around the wall. *Okay. It looks like we have to play 'match the faces' before they change,* he thought to himself.

He chose a face from the parchment; then his eyes darted across the ones in front of him as they morphed in the shifting candlelight. There! In the centre. One that matched. He quickly reached out and touched its crooked nose. There was a soft *click* and the face morphed into an impish smile.

'Aha!' he announced. 'Just got to be quick, that's all.'

He studied the next face on his clue, and then looked back at the stone grid. He spotted a match in the bottom right-hand corner, but just as his fingers reached it, its image changed. He scanned them again, the matching face appeared to his left, and this time he was quick enough. Once again, as he touched it, the features changed into a fixed smile.

'Four to go,' he whispered, as he licked his dry lips.

With steady perseverance, he managed to match another three. It took him a while, as the candle now burned low and the flickering seemed only to speed up the changing expressions. Now, seven shifting stone faces stared defiantly back at him.

'Right, number six, where are you?'

No matter how fast he was, the final matching face avoided him. It seemed to Frog that it taunted him, flitting away in a nanosecond, just as his fingers reached tantalisingly close to it. He tried to second-guess where it would appear. He tried following a pattern. He tried counting to see if there was a regular sequence. None of it worked. The candle burned down to a spluttering stub.

'Come on. Come on,' he complained.

His patience was being tested, and his eyes were feeling strained in the shifting light. In a final flurry of frustration, he clenched his fists and struck the gothic-looking faces.

'I. HATE. PUZZLES!' he shouted.

He gave one particular image, which had a rudely extended tongue, a furious thump, which he immediately regretted as a sharp pain ricocheted up his wrist.

'Yeow!'

He looked on as blood oozed from a gash in the side of his hand. In an effort to stem the bleeding and relieve the pain, he pushed the wound up to his mouth and sucked on the cut. He gave the offending face a look of anger, only to be surprised that its expression had changed to a grin.

'Oh. Very funny,' he remarked.

In the silence, he heard the rough scraping of stone on stone.

'Now what?'

There was a muffled *thud*. That was when the floor beneath him dissolved, and he dropped with all the elegance of a sack of potatoes into a narrow tunnel. His body connected with the smooth, slippery surface of polished stone, and he hurtled down a rock-hewn flume into the unknown.

He slid out onto a soft, earth floor; to rest spread-eagled on his back. As he lay there, regaining his breath, he stared up at a myriad of dust motes, which danced around in narrow beams of light, as if to an unheard melody,

And that's why I really hate puzzles, he thought to himself.

He raised himself up on one elbow and focussed his eyes on his surroundings to find that he was in a small, circular cave, just large enough for him to stand up in.

Veins of silver and copper-coloured crystal rippled in the rock walls, and narrow streaks of light played across the reflective surfaces. The source of the light was on the opposite side of the cave.

He caught his breath. There, growing out of the rock, was a golden tree no more than half a metre tall – the Tree of Spells.

Thin strands of light reached out from its branches like rays of sunshine from behind evening clouds. The Tree was encompassed by a transparent orb, which shimmered pale blue thread-like patterns across its gossamer surface. Frog moved closer and he tentatively reached his hand out; his index finger trembled slightly as he touched the orb. In a blink, it turned to a solid ball of stone. The Tree of Spells was now encased inside of the immovable and unbreakable rock.

'I had to touch. Why didn't I just look first?' he scolded himself.

As he pondered over what he should do next, Frog noticed a distinct hollow shape set in the base of the rock shelf.

He opened his pouch and took out the crystal. Gently, he placed it into the empty shape; it fitted perfectly like the precise piece of a jigsaw. He knelt and watched with awe and relief as the ball of rock became transparent again and then dissolved. The unprotected Tree of Spells shone in wondrous glory, and in response, Frog's forehead glowed golden with the Light of the Chosen.

In that peaceful moment, Frog felt a connection, an understanding that something had just passed between the Tree of Spells and himself.

The Mountain shook. A violent vibration disturbed the calm. The cave trembled and juddered; loose rocks fell from above and clattered to the floor in plumes of dust. A large crack snaked across the ceiling, and a jagged hole appeared from which a smoke-like cloud wound its way into the cave, to form the shape of a pulsating black hand. It wrapped itself around the Tree and wrenched it upwards. Frog could see the Tree's roots straining against the force that threatened to pull it from the rock, and in desperation, he lunged forwards to grasp its trunk.

'Noooo!' he shouted.

'The Tree of Spells is mine!' boomed a deep and threatening voice. 'None shall stop me now.'

The Tree came free and its golden roots were exposed. Frog hung on in a desperate tug-of-war as it was pulled towards the opening in the roof. The black, billowing hand jerked the Tree violently from side to side, but still Frog kept his grip, holding on for all his life with both fists. With a twist and a tear, the bottom of the Tree split and separated, and a chorus of screaming and despairing voices filled the air. The trunk and its branches disappeared up into the ceiling, gripped in the clenched fist of black vapour. As Frog fell to the floor, the mangled roots of the Tree in his hand, the terrible and triumphant voice of Lord Maelstrom thundered in the air around him.

'I am invincible, the Tree of Spells is mine, and all of its powers belong to me. Soon I will venture to your world, boy, where I will destroy everything and everyone who you love. Then I shall return for you – I will drag whatever is left of your miserable existence to the desolation that was your home. You shall witness my revenge, and all that will be left to greet you will be the deathly remains of all that you once knew…'

The cave continued to shake, the walls crumbled inwards, and the ceiling collapsed. Rocks rained their crushing weight down onto Frog. All that he could do was curl himself into a ball and wait for death to claim him.

However, death did not come. Beneath the mound of rock and debris, he held the roots of the Tree of Spells; their magic surrounded him with a protective shield, a cocoon of energy. Frog opened his eyes to the blue-white light that shone around him. He had been saved, but it would appear that he was also imprisoned, buried deep within the heart of Black Mountain, whilst far away, Tropal went to war, and Lord Maelstrom possessed the Tree of Spells.

36.

The Battle for Tropal

The day blinked away, and an unhealthy yellow moon appeared in the sky. Under the stare of its sickly feverish light, the black veins of Lord Maelstrom's army swept out from the caves and tunnels of Black Mountain. Creatures of the underworld, living and dead, surged forwards in a great clamour of screams, shrieks and roars. The beat of unseen drums echoed out before them like rolling thunder. Ragged black flags flapped from tall poles, fixed and strapped to enormous, lumbering centipede-like creatures; skeletal shapes rode their scaly backs, urging them forwards with vicious lashes from long flame-edged whips.

The eyes of this multitude were as black as coal, as were the hearts of those that might have possessed such a beating thing. Mostly, they were borne of the vilest magic that Lord Maelstrom's corrupt thoughts could create. They were incarnations of the foulest nightmares. They sought only to kill and to destroy anything of beauty, of courage or of goodness. Their own annihilation did not disturb them; they felt no pain and the only fear they knew was that of Lord Maelstrom. They existed only to serve his will.

The throng swarmed along the base of Black Mountain. They spread out like a black stain onto the Flatlands, and with them came the stench of death and decay. Teams of huge ash-grey lizards pulled war chariots, which overflowed with monstrous, red-eyed rats, their yellow, decaying teeth protruding, vampire-like, from their mouths.

The army of Tropal watched unmoved from across the plains. No mind wavered from its task. No heart sank in despair. They stood strong and resolute.

Along the front of its battle line stood twenty-four pure white Griffin, half lion, half eagle, and on each one sat a member of the Council with the Guardian at their midst.

Their chant began as a low murmur. 'Let the Light deliver us from evil.'

It spread through the ranks, until in thousands of voices, the words echoed out over the Flatlands.

'Let the Light deliver us from evil.'

'Let the Light deliver us from evil.'

'Let the Light deliver us from evil.'

The side of Black Mountain exploded with such force and noise that all those upon the plain turned their human and inhuman eyes in its direction.

Rock and dust tumbled down, and smoke clouds billowed out from a cavernous hole, which blazed blood red from within.

A giant of a figure, nearly thirty metres high, came floating out on a pulsating green cloud, which hovered high above the Flatlands. Those who possessed a soul turned away as their stomachs and minds reeled at the hideous thing Lord Maelstrom had become. What was brought into the world in human form was now the image and substance of unimaginable horror. His night-black cloak billowed out in long, torn tendrils upon which, agonised faces shifted, their mouths open in cries of torment. His arms spread out wide, and in each fist he gripped the mangled remains of the Tree of Spells.

His voice hissed and bubbled into the minds of all. None could escape its venomous message.

'Behold! The Tree of Spells is mine. I am Lord Maelstrom! Say my name in terror for I shall rule you all. The Dimensions shall fall beneath my feet and so shall all those other worlds; those specks of light in the sky, until they are extinguished and nothing but endless dark remains. One by one, the Guardians shall fall against my will. They are powerless to stop me now. Even your Chosen one cannot save you.'

There was a moment's silence as if even time feared to move on; then with one deafening accord, Tropal's people's voices rose up in defiance.

'Let the Light deliver us from evil.'

A wide slash of torn skin on Lord Maelstrom's face, where his mouth should have been, shaped itself into a cruel smile.

'Your Light grows weak. It fails you. Nothing can protect you now.' It seemed that the very air was poisoned by the sound of his voice. 'Prepare to meet your doom!'

The mountain itself came under Lord Maelstrom's control. From its summit, great fiery clusters of burning embers and lava spewed into the sky, arcing out in trails of blazing comets towards the army of Tropal.

Both armies launched themselves forwards, on a collision course of good against evil, of survival or annihilation. Bravery, courage and fearlessness waded into the carnage on the faces and shoulders of Tropal's multitude.

In that precious moment, Fate became a throw of tumbling cosmic dice.

The line of Griffin bound valiantly forwards to meet the front rows of spear-wielding creatures head on. At the last moment they flapped their great-feathered wings and soared above the black tide, to swipe their talons at the foul heads and scythe them from their bodies, which fell lifeless, to be trampled on and ground into the earth by the feet of countless others. The Griffin riders fired poisonous darts from their blowpipes; so precise was their aim that none missed their targets.

Fireballs dropped indiscriminately from the sky and incinerated scores of human and inhuman forms. Flaming arrows rained down with evil poison on their tips, which burrowed like cockroaches through armour and delivered instant death to all that it reached.

The two armies merged into a writhing, fighting mass. Here and there, pockets of forest people became isolated only to be enveloped and swarmed over by venomous creatures. Amidst what had now become a free-for-all, a new threat emerged – the monstrous Drak. They waded forwards with their long green tentacles reaching out to crush the life's breath from their prey.

As the battle raged on, the Guardian turned his Griffin back to the forest's edge, where a second wave of his people waited impatiently.

'Now!' he commanded. 'Now is the moment!'

High in the trees, branches were pulled back to reveal great catapults, loaded with pulsating globes of colour. The taut ropes were released and orbs of swirling rainbows streaked out. They burst open above the soulless creatures and sprayed out their contents like multi-coloured rain. Colours melted into everything that it fell upon, and the effect was like a rapidly spreading virus. Lord Maelstrom's creations began to fall, writhing onto the ground, the colours melting their shapes into harmless pools of rainbow-like liquid. Any Drak that were hit by the missile's explosions of vibrant tints and shades, stumbled to a halt before greens and browns covered their forms and they became rooted into the earth, transformed into harmless trees.

The Guardian swooped and wheeled overhead astride his Griffin. His staff delivered jagged lightning bolts at the largest of the abominable creatures, which turned to ash and allowed Tropal's fighters the freedom to move in and defeat the smaller ones.

For a while, the army of Tropal appeared to be overpowering Lord Maelstrom's legion; some of the lesser creations began to falter and hesitate as the bombardment of colour-filled orbs continued to fall and destroy those around them.

Above the clamour of battle, Lord Maelstrom's voice boomed out to rent the air like a jagged knife.

'Guardian! Do you think that you have won? Enjoy your short victory. I grow tired of these pathetic games, and I am restless to claim a bigger prize – a Dimension that will give me the greatest satisfaction of all to crush and consign into the realms of oblivion. Now that I have the Tree of Spells, only you and your kind stand like weak saplings in the path of my domination.

'I go to Terrae, the Fourth Dimension, where I shall destroy humanity, and quench my revenge. Let all of the Guardians come and face me there, to bow down and be witness to my supremacy.

'I shall leave you here with something special. I am rather proud of this creation, for they are as hungry as I am for your misery and despair.'

He brought his arms over his head, and crushed the pieces of the Tree of Spells between his hands. A spinning vortex churned above him – the Slipstream opened and Lord Maelstrom slid effortlessly into it, before it closed with a crack of unearthly thunder.

The green cloud, on which he had been standing, turned black, and billowed out with the threat of an oncoming storm. It rolled across the Flatlands, curling out like stagnant, murky water. Then came the rain. Fat oily droplets that fell in a torrent and washed away any trace of colour. The ground became a glutinous swamp that sucked and cloyed at feet and legs.

When the rain stopped, it was to herald another onslaught of evil. A rustling sound filled the air, like dead autumn leaves being scattered by the wind, and from the dark clouds, a swarm of fluttering wings descended. Harpies! Small, evil-looking, fairy-like beings with long spiteful faces and needle-sharp teeth. Teeth with the power to inject despair and misery into their victims, and enough fear to make the bravest person curl themselves up into a ball and lose their sanity.

They fell upon Tropal's army like locusts on a field of corn, and the Guardian looked on in a despair of his own.

'Fall back! Fall back!' he cried. 'To the cover of the trees.'

Over half of Tropal's army, human and animal, did not reach the shelter of the forest in time, before the Guardian threw up a protective curtain of humming blue power from his staff. A few of the Harpies threw themselves at the barrier in blind spite, but they crackled and hissed on contact to fall dead to the floor, like flies against an electric fluorescent flytrap. Seeing the consequences, the majority of them flew back to perch gargoyle-like on the quivering, cowered bodies of their victims.

The rest of Lord Maelstrom's legions gathered in deep ranks as close as they dared, watching for any sign of weakness in the barrier, waiting for the opportunity to flood into the forest and overwhelm the outnumbered army of Tropal.

Only twelve of the Council remained, and they gathered around the Guardian.

'We have failed,' said one. 'The forest will be overrun and destroyed. Tropal will be no more.'

'Our only option is to retreat deep into the secret places, and save ourselves,' suggested another.

'Will they not accept terms of surrender?' pleaded a young and injured fighter.

From amongst the dread-induced babble, one voice spoke up. It was Gabe. He stood bloodied and torn, but upright and proud.

'Just listen to yourselves. You shame Tropal. You

shame your fallen people! Did you really think that the task would be easy? Did you not consider that victory and honour might also be in death? There can be no surrender. There will be nowhere to hide. The only answer to our freedom lies out there, to fight with dignity and destroy as much evil while we still have breath in our bodies. Listen to me, I have hope, I have a plan, and it may buy us time.'

'Time? Time for what?' challenged a voice. 'The Horsemen are not coming. They have deserted us. We are alone.'

'Then alone we shall stand, together. If not for ourselves, but for the Chosen one and for Jorge and Mystra, and all of those who have given their lives today. Or, would you rather that history remember you as those who ran away? Not I. I would ask the Guardian to lower the barrier and let me walk out there, alone if necessary, to at least die trying.'

Humbled, they let his words echo within their heads.

In time, a voice spoke up. 'Together it shall be, then.'

'*All* must agree,' said the Guardian. 'Are we as one?'

A while later, the Guardian stepped out from the tree line, his staff held out in front of him. The blue curtain of energy moved forwards as he walked into the open, and as the barrier shifted, so the clawing, hissing creatures scrabbled menacingly backwards.

In the spreading space of the Guardian's barrier, the remnants of Tropal's army emerged to form a circular group of defiance. There were now no more than five hundred of them. Their faces were hardened and bold, and the forest colours of greens and browns flickered and shifted brightly across their bodies.

They gripped their shields, lances and swords, ready for close combat, ready to fight one last time, and they were not afraid to look into the eyes of their enemies.

'There are so many of them, and so few of us,' remarked one of the Council.

'Then all the greater the victory that awaits us,' said another, with renewed optimism.

Gabe turned to the Guardian. 'It should be daylight by now.'

The Guardian glanced up at the cloud-blackened sky. 'Somewhere above, the sun still shines. Now, take your place. The moment has come to do our duty.'

Gabe climbed up the stout trunk of one of the great trees, and he walked out onto a mighty overhanging branch.

'On my signal,' the Guardian nodded.

He continued to move forwards, the small army following him, heads held high. The Guardian's magic shield enveloped them in a protective bubble as they pushed into the mass of Lord Maelstrom's hoards. While the barrier existed neither they nor their enemies could reach each other. Some of the vile creatures, impatient for blood, threw themselves forwards, only to explode in a shower of sparks and black dust.

Further and further, the group pushed, until they were in the midst of the Flatlands and totally surrounded by the hoard of frenzied creatures.

'Prepare!' commanded the Guardian.

Weapons were readied, shields were raised, and they became a covered dome, their lances pushed out through small gaps, which gave the impression of a great spike-covered tortoiseshell. At its centre, the Guardian stood exposed. He thrust his staff into the ground, and the blue-white barrier rolled back to form a rippling column of energy that twisted and spun like a cyclone. It reached upwards to touch the black clouds, and burst a hole through to reveal a clear white-bleached sky. As the cloud cover melted away, the sun itself was revealed in its shining purple radiance.

The creatures screamed and wailed; they clawed at their own eyes in sudden blindness. The Harpies, however, seemed unaffected and they rose up in swarms of fury to attack the shielded assembly. Their mass was so great that they cast pools of shadows below them, enough for black twisted beasts to regain their eyesight and launch their assault.

The Harpies scrabbled over the shielded army,

clawing and tearing, trying to force their way into Tropal's fighters, and cause havoc and despair.

As the cloud cover melted further away, the sound of a hunting horn echoed out from Gabe's lips to summon another more colourful swarm, which swept out of the forest to descend upon the Harpies. The bold, brown and white mountain eagles and the multi-coloured birds of the forest, their bright plumage vivid in the sunlight, swooped down to peck and claw at the host of Harpies, which became overwhelmed and torn from their dreadful mission.

The front row of shields moved forwards and the circle of defence expanded outwards. Row upon row of forest fighters moved from the core and filled the gaps, lances and swords thrusting out, bringing down their attackers. As the sun cast its warmth across the ground, all those who had been affected by the Harpies now awoke revitalised by a bright new energy. They shook their heads, and regained their senses, quickly picking up their weapons to fight with a new vigour, alongside their companions.

Gabe ran from the trees towards the fight with his sword poised high in his hand, only to falter. His face blanched as he saw yet another wave of terror descend from Black Mountain. Monstrous flying things with long spear-like beaks and wide leathery wings, their tips clawed and hooked with barbs ready to snatch and tear at their enemy.

The first of the winged beasts dropped earthwards on its mission to deliver inevitable carnage and death. It beat its wings to slow its approach and its sharp talons reached out to grasp its prey.

With the silence and speed of Death's scythe, the long, black-feathered shaft of an arrow pierced the side of its head, and with shocked, bulging eyes, it crashed to the ground, crushing many of the black army beneath its foul hulk in the process.

A flurry of arrows sang through the air at more of the flying creatures, and Gabe turned his gaze towards the source of the unexpected reinforcements.

Thundering across the Flatlands and into the battle came the Horsemen of Tropal. Now restored to their human form, they rode their magnificent horses, bedecked in battle armour and armed with their mighty bows and spears. They trampled into the fight with overwhelming vengeance and fury.

Lord Maelstrom's army became unravelled and disorganised. Many of them turned on their own kind in a final act of wanton evil before they were themselves cut down.

As the Horsemen surged into the melee, Gabe caught sight of his dearest friend Jorge, sword in hand, sitting astride a young, black colt. For a moment their eyes connected and they exchanged affectionate smiles, before a wave of tumbling, thrashing creatures distracted them both back into the heart of combat.

Much later, in the smoking stillness and aftermath of the battle, Gabe would be reunited with his friend Jorge, only this time Dagar would carry Jorge's pale, lifeless body in his arms and lay him solemnly at Gabe's feet.

'Would that I possessed half of the courage and loyalty of this boy,' said Dagar. 'His name shall forever be spoken with great affection and respect amongst my people.'

The army of Tropal suffered many losses that day. Only ten of the Council survived. Countless animals and forest people lay dead or mortally injured, and the Guardian almost diminished his powers in his efforts to heal and cure as many as he was able.

The remnants of Lord Maelstrom's legions that were strewn across the Flatlands were, without exception, finally destroyed by the Guardian's magic. That same magic was called upon to cleanse the lands of any remains of the unearthly creations.

During and after the battle, the Guardian had constantly reached out to try to connect with Frog's mind. There was nothing, and he pondered how the future would unfold now that Lord Maelstrom possessed the Tree of Spells. He resigned to the fact that the Chosen one was lost. The prophecy of old was flawed, and Frog was dead or imprisoned in some bleak existence under Lord Maelstrom's will. An uncertain future loomed ahead.

37.

SPIDER

Deep within the heart of Black Mountain, beneath a mound of rocks and debris, Frog considered his fate. He placed the palms of his hands against the inside of the glowing blue orb; its surface felt like cool glass. Fragments of energy skittered across its shell like tiny lightning storms.

Frog sat back on his heels, and his hair stood out as if energised by static. On the floor in front of him lay the tangled, golden remains of the Tree of Spell's roots. He surveyed the salvation that had become his prison.

'Well,' he breathed in. 'I certainly made a mess of that. Didn't I?'

Frustration bubbled to the surface. He looked up and held his hands out in a gesture of bewilderment.

'Is this it? Is this where it all ends?' Then anger rose like a red mist across his eyes. 'What was the point? The Chosen one? Don't make me laugh.' His voice became bitter and mocking. 'Guardians!

Where are you now? Destiny? Ha! You haven't got a clue! Fate? There's no such thing.'

He took in a deep breath to savour his bitterness and disappointment, and then he carried on with his one-sided conversation.

'Now. Let's just recap, shall we? Come to Tropal, they said. Find the Tree of Spells. Save us from Lord Maelstrom, they said. I came, endured some pretty unpleasant and painful experiences, lost another good friend in the process, and despite my best efforts, for all I know, everything and everyone that I love is being destroyed, while I'm trapped beneath a pile of rocks!'

He beat at the sides of the orb with his fists as he struggled to fight off angry tears.

'Dimensions. Guardians. Magic. Why me? What have I done to deserve this? Why have I been deserted? Why am I alone? Answer me. Answer me!' He shouted with anger and frustration.

His shoulders sagged as he leant forwards and dropped his hands into his lap. His fury spent, tears finally escaped to run like raindrops down his face and chin. They dripped into his upturned palms in a tiny pool of precious sorrow.

In that moment, in the silence of sadness, a familiar voice drifted into his head.

Things are not always —

Frog raised his face and spoke in sobs of

resentment. 'Oh! Not that again. Things are not always as they seem. How many more times must I hear that? It's getting boring now!'

The voice of Gizmo, the old Guardian from Castellion, continued in Frog's head.

I was going to say that things are not always that simple. Life is not easy. No journey is without its challenges and disappointments; that is what makes success all the more rewarding. Sometimes you can sit back and enjoy the ride – other times you have to get out and push! The universe, or whatever we choose to call it, continues to surprise us. Now and then, we find help in the most unlikely places. Despite your doubts, you have never been alone.

Frog felt a tingling sensation ripple around his wrist, and he looked down to see that the black spider tattoo on his skin had once again become a solid metal bracelet.

Well? A girl's familiar voice entered his head. *Are you going to let me out?*

With trembling fingers, Frog flipped back the centre of the bracelet to reveal the spindly-legged spider that he had last seen in his home Dimension. The little creature stretched its micro-thin legs, until it stood with all the confidence of an accomplished stilt walker.

Hi! Along with the word, the image of a smile appeared in Frog's head. *Need some help?*

Frog reached out to the spider with his mind. *Sure.* He smiled back as he gave a soggy sniff. *Sorry,* he apologised. He wiped his tear-wet face with the back of his arm. *I just felt so alone and helpless.*

You're not alone, and you're not helpless. Just remember who you are. Now, place me on the ground.

Frog gently cupped the spider in his palm and then allowed it to crawl onto the dusty floor.

I shan't be long. Do you think that you'll be okay for a while longer?

Sure, Frog replied. *I'm not going anywhere.*

Glad to see that you've still got your sense of humour. See you soon.

The spider made its way to the edge of the orb, and without any hesitation, it passed right through and into the darkness beyond.

Optimism crept back into Frog's senses, and he knelt patiently, waiting for the spider's return.

Time passed. He had no way of knowing how long. He drew strength from the fact that he had not been forgotten, and that in some small way the power of the Guardians still reached out to him. But were they too late? How was he supposed to fight Lord Maelstrom now that he had lost the Tree of Spells?

As he pondered and contemplated on so many unknown issues, a small stain of red appeared on the surface of the globe, just above his head. Then another patch to the right of him followed, then another to his left. The darkness outside seemed to be falling away, until eventually, a red glow merged with the blue light of the orb to bathe him in a purple aura. He looked on with fascination as the orb swirled in a myriad of clouds, which then melted away to leave a warm crimson light. He was free.

The avalanche of rocks that had covered him had been pulled back, cleared to the edges of the cave. He picked out a shadowed figure, and as his eyes adjusted, he caught his breath at the sight of the smiling face staring back at him.

'Mystra!'

He scrabbled to his feet and rushed to her. He wrapped his arms around her and buried his head in her shoulder, and she embraced him back. Unashamed tears of his happiness wet her hair.

'I thought that you were dead,' he said, finally pulling himself back to allow his eyes to drink in her smile.

'So did I. If you hadn't given me the gift of the Chosen, I'm sure that I would have been.'

'What happened? Where did you go?'

'Let's just say that Oblivion is a cold and dark place,' she replied. 'I fell into darkness, sort of found myself floating in it. At first, I panicked. I was screaming and shouting. When I realised that I was alone and no one was going to come, I tried calling out with my mind. To begin with, there was nothing, not a sound. Then I heard your voice and those words.'

'I reached out to you,' said Frog. 'I called your name, but nothing came back.'

'I didn't hear you calling my name,' she said. 'Just the words.'

'What words?'

"Let the Light deliver us from evil." She paused. 'I started to repeat it over and over, out loud. Gradually, a golden glow shone from my forehead; then I felt solid ground beneath my feet, so I started walking. The darkness always seemed to be just ahead of me, and I thought that I was destined to walk forever. All of a sudden, I realised that I was in a tunnel with rock walls around me, so I just followed it and hoped that it would lead me out. I don't know how long I was wandering around. I do remember at one point that I felt really tired and I fell asleep. A girl's voice woke me up, but the voice was in my head. At first, I thought that I was having a waking dream, until she explained about you, and what had happened. Her voice guided me here and she told me to move the rocks to let you out.'

See. I told you that you weren't alone. The spider spoke in Frog's head.

'Did you hear that?' said Mystra. 'It's her voice!'

'I know,' said Frog. 'She's my friend.'

Over here. The spider guided Frog to the side of the cave, where she hung by a single thread.

Frog held out his hand and she clambered on to his palm.

Time to go. There is a new passageway behind you. It will lead you out of the mountain. Now, you must put me back inside the bracelet.

Frog placed the spider into the small compartment.

Will we meet again? asked Frog.

Who knows? she replied. *One more thing, young Frog. Do not forget what you came here for.*

The Tree of Spells has gone, he said.

But not the roots! They are yours to protect. Do not lose them. Take them to the Guardian. Now, close the lid.

Mystra stared with wonder as the bracelet melted into Frog's skin to become the spider tattoo once again.

'At least I managed to save something,' Frog said, as he gently picked up the mangled roots from the floor. 'Though what good they will be, compared to the powers that the Dark Lord has taken, is another mystery.'

He carefully placed them into the safety of his pouch.

'Mystra. I need to get home to my own world. That's where *he's* going, and if there's anything left that I can do to stop him, then that's where I must be, with my family. With the people that I love. We have to find the Guardian.'

Mystra took his hand. 'Come on. As fearful as I am, we first have to find out what has happened to Tropal, to my people. To my world.'

38.

TIME

Two days had passed since the battle, when Frog and Mystra emerged from the mouth of a cave and out onto the side of Black Mountain. Spread out before them were the Flatlands, now deserted and barren. In many places, the ground bore the charred black scars of fire – the only indication that something destructive had happened there.

'Can you smell that?' asked Mystra.

Frog sniffed at the air. 'Smoke, and something else.'

'Death,' she said, flatly.

Neither of them felt like talking as they made their way down the mountainside, and by the time that they had crossed the Flatlands and reached the edge of the forest, night had fallen.

Mystra paused as they stepped warily under the great boughs.

'Listen!' she whispered.

'What?' Frog went to draw his sword.

'No!' She stopped him. 'It's the forest. You can hear it breathing. It's unharmed. The forest has been saved!'

She ran ahead, recklessly, throwing her arms in the air, spinning around and dancing with joy. Even in the shadowed light, Frog could see the colours on her skin rippling like liquid fireworks.

'Come on! The Canopy must be only a couple of hours away.'

Frog chased after her, elated and energised by her excitement. 'Wait for me!'

Eventually, their energy waned and they slowed to a walking pace, enjoying the peace and tranquillity of the forest. As they walked side by side, Mystra slipped her hand into Frog's and felt the deep comfort and delight of their friendship.

In the early hours, just before dawn, they caught sight of the warm, glowing lights of the Canopy, which seemed to welcome them through the trees.

'Home,' sighed Mystra.

They pushed their way out of the low foliage and into the clearing; small glowing lights like summer fireflies began to float down and fill the air. Glittering sparks danced around them as if the very stars had been sent to greet them. As they stood there, their upturned faces bathed in wonder. The people of the Canopy appeared above them; they crowded along the walkways and filled the balconies.

A soft melody rose up and drifted through the air;

harmonies swirled from countless voices as a song of the forest wound its way through the trees and branches. Frog felt that he was in a dream; his heart swelled with joy and his head became light with emotion. He could not understand the words, but the ancient language reached right into his very soul and made him want to laugh and cry with pleasure.

When the singing stopped, and as the last words echoed and faded away like the remnants of a dream, the Guardian stepped from the gentleness of the shadows. Although he smiled and was overjoyed at their survival, Frog noticed that he also looked careworn and tired.

'Welcome. I must admit that there was a moment when even I thought that you had both been lost. I searched out with my mind many times, but the power of Black Mountain concealed you from me.'

'Oh! You don't know the half of it,' said Frog. 'That mountain has a lot to answer for!'

The Guardian smiled again. 'I'm sure that you will tell me all. And we have much to discuss.'

'I want to go home,' said Frog. 'That's where I need to be. I'm not going to wait for him to come and get me after he has destroyed everything that I love. I want to be there, to face him. I'm sorry about the Tree of Spells. There was nothing more that I could have done.'

The Guardian placed his hand gently on Frog's shoulder. 'You have done all that needed to have been done. The hour is indeed near for your return, but before I let you go there are things that you need to know. However, firstly you must say your goodbyes.' He nodded at Mystra. 'Starting here and now.'

Frog turned to her. For a moment, he chewed at his lip. He didn't want to look into her eyes. He had known the pain of losing her already, and memories of leaving others in the past, whom he had become very fond of, overwhelmed his thoughts.

In the end, it was Mystra who spoke.

'I have feelings for you that go beyond friendship,' she said, quietly. 'I'm sure that if it were any other place or time, we would have such a future together. But that is not meant to be.'

Frog summoned up the courage to look her in the face, even though his throat had become as dry as a desert wind. Tears hung on her eyelashes and lights reflected in the wetness of her eyes. He opened his mouth to say words that had not even formed in his mind.

She stopped him. 'Don't! Please don't say anything.' She placed a warm finger across his lips. 'I shall never forget you.'

Before he could react, she turned, and without looking back, she walked towards a group of waiting friends and family, their arms open to surround her in their warm embrace. That was last that he saw of her.

The Guardian's arm wrapped around Frog's shoulder, as a comforting friend, and he guided him towards a stairway, which led to the Cradle. As they made their way up and along the walkways of the Canopy, the Guardian spoke gently, and his words softened Frog's pain and the regret he already held of not saying the things that he now wished to say to Mystra.

They briefly stopped at a hut, where Frog found his whip and his old clothes folded neatly on a chair, and as he changed back into them, the Guardian spoke of the battle, of Jorge's death, of the loss of many, and of the task ahead. Frog recalled the image of Jorge's smiling face, and mentally, he folded up another little parcel of sadness, in memory of their short friendship.

'All is not lost, young Frog,' the Guardian said as they crossed the narrow bridge and stepped into the Cradle. 'The Dark Lord cannot enter your Dimension yet. He is in Limbo and it is there that he will make his preparations. Until you return, only then will the Slipstream allow him passage. He does not know it, but you still hold the key to his downfall.'

'What? How?'

'Reach into your pouch and take out the two items that remain.'

Frog brought the objects out and held them in his palms. In one rested the crumpled, golden roots of the Tree of Spells, and in the other was the compass.

'Come. It is time. Stand on the dais and face the moon,' instructed the Guardian. 'Hold the objects out in your hands and close your eyes.'

Frog did as he was told. He sensed that something more than his return through the Slipstream was about to happen. Above the moon, three bright stars flashed with a blue-white brilliance that burst their image through Frog's eyelids and flooded his mind.

'Orion's belt,' he gasped.

Three rippling strands of blue plasma reached out from the stars across the sky and connected with Frog. One to his forehead, one to the roots, and one to the compass.

A vortex formed around him, and his clothes billowed restlessly in the airstream. The dark green material of his attire was suddenly bleached the brightest of white. For a few moments, his mind was flooded with the ancient knowledge of time itself.

The wind subsided to the gentleness of a summer breeze, and everything returned to normal as if a curtain had been drawn back on the morning of a calm and clear day. It was indeed daybreak; Tropal's purple sun hovered in the sky and orange clouds drifted lazily along as if scattered there by some unseen artistic hand.

Although his clothes had returned to their

normal green colouring, the difference was in Frog himself: his hair had become the darkest of blacks, and streaks of burnished gold ran through it in clusters of fine threads. His eyes, once green, now shone blue with the power of the Chosen.

He turned to the Guardian. 'What happened? I feel different.'

The Guardian reached out a finger and drew an oval in the air, and in it, Frog saw a reflection of himself.

'What? Oh, man! My Mum's going to kill me!' He ran his fingers through his hair as if he could rub the transformation away. 'And look at my eyes!' He leaned forwards for a closer inspection. 'Tell me what's happened?'

'You have inherited the power of the Tree of Spells.'

'But Lord Maelstrom's taken that. He's got all the powers. I just managed to save the roots, which by the way appear to have melted into my hair!' He tugged at the black and golden locks.

'He *thinks* that he has all of the powers.' The Guardian smiled. 'The most important power of all was concealed in the roots, and as the Chosen one, that power has passed to you.'

'So, what *have* I got?'

Frog looked down at the hand that held the compass; the shape of the object remained the same, but it now resembled some form of timepiece.

'You have the power to control and change time itself,' declared the Guardian.

'Is that what this does?'

'It is a Time Shifter, and it will work only through your will, in your hands, by your command. It gives you the ability to be in one place or in many places at the same time – you can control the Paradox.'

'If I remember rightly,' said Frog, 'a Paradox is supposed to be a scientific impossibility.'

'You must remember, my young friend, that here we are dealing with nature, with the forces of creation itself. Science has nothing to do with it.'

Frog inspected the Time Shifter. 'So how exactly does it work?'

'You already know. That knowledge has always been buried deep within you. Go on,' encouraged the Guardian. 'Try it. Set it to take you home.'

Instinctively, Frog turned the dials until the needles were set in the right positions. He studied it for a moment. 'That's weird how something in my head tells me how to do that. What happens now?'

The Guardian's kindly face stared down at him. 'Your journey here is over, and a new one awaits you. With it, there will be many revelations. Mysteries are unfolding as we speak, and magic older than the dawn of time awakens in the multiverse. Soon, in your world, the fate of the past, the present and the future, across *all* Dimensions, shall be decided through your actions and your decisions.'

'Why me? Why has it always been me? That's what I don't understand.'

'Some may call it Fate. Others would believe it to be destiny. The true answer, my friend, flows in your blood and lives in the past, but the past is returning to shape the future. Let us hope that it is a future that will free us all from evil.'

'Life seemed so much simpler when I was just an ordinary boy.'

'You were *never* an ordinary boy. Now go. Your home is waiting, and don't worry, whilst you have been away, nothing bad has happened to those who you love.'

As he smiled a goodbye to the Guardian, Frog held the Time Shifter against his chest. This time, the whirling, cosmic turbulence of the Slipstream did not open up. There was no movement. No falling sensation. Everything around him just faded away in a bright, all-consuming light. When nothing was left, and a wall of pure white enveloped him, the light began to dim, and new surroundings took shape, until once more he viewed the familiar landscape of an orchard. He was home.

The air was warm and humid, and a full moon

hung majestically in the summer night sky. He smiled as his eyes picked out the constellation of Orion; its silver beacons flickered in the vastness of space.

It took him a few seconds before he realised that something was wrong. With the Slipstream, only a second or two separated the Dimensions, and on past journeys time in his world stood still whilst he was away.

'It's night-time,' he mouthed as he surveyed the starry sky. 'I left in daylight. Oh. This is not good.'

He sensed that something else was different. Time here had indeed moved on since he had left for Tropal. How long that had been, he had no idea, only that there was the possibility that his absence may well have been discovered.

He made his way to the shed, and he couldn't help but notice that all of the lights in his house were on. 'Oh! Not good. Definitely not good.' he repeated, as he shook his head.

Inside the shed, he changed back into his jeans, t-shirt and trainers. His Frog clothes and other Dimensional belongings, including the Time Shifter, were bundled up and hidden in the drawer of the old dresser. All the while, he was trying to form a plausible untruth to tell whichever of his parents, if not both, should they be waiting to confront him when he entered the house.

Everything that he considered ran around his head like an errant, bouncing rubber ball.

I've been around Billy's – no good. The first thing that they would have done was phoned there to check.

I went for a walk – what? At this time of night!

I was abducted by aliens! Now you're getting desperate!

He was still running numerous ridiculous excuses through his head as he pushed open the back door and walked into the empty kitchen.

Nervously, he called out. 'Mum? Dad?'

'In here, Chris.' It was his mother's voice, from the lounge.

With leaden feet, Chris walked down the hallway towards the open door. He paused briefly to examine his reflection in the hall mirror. To his relief he looked his normal self. No black and gold hair, no bright blue eyes.

He entered the room to be greeted by his mother and father, who were seated side by side on the sofa.

'Welcome home, Chris,' said his mum. The expression on her face was far from welcoming.

'Well, Christopher,' said his dad.

Oh, Man! Thought Chris. *He used my whole name. I am in sooo much trouble.*

'Sit down, young man,' his dad continued. 'You have a lot of explaining to do.'

EPILOGUE

A force rippled through the Slipstream; it reached out across the Dimensions to three Guardians. Gizmo, Guardian of Castellion; Cassaria, Guardian of Aridian; and Koy, Guardian of Tropal. Its power also reached a fourth, sleeping Guardian, who stirred quietly in their slumber. Soon, they would be called together, across time and space, to a place where the future and fate of all good peoples and worlds shall be decided.

Powers of control, wisdom, and cunning will be the weapons. Dark forces, black arts and ancient evils will face white magic, mystic powers and faith.

At the heart of it all sits one boy whose journey began well before he was born. He has many names. Chris and Frog are just two of them. The mysterious powers of time flow through his bloodline, and so flow through his own veins also. He has always been destined to carry the fate of the multiverse. Unaware of his importance, he was born as the most human of children, protected by secrets, until one evening, the past unfolded and reached out for him, knowing who and what he really was.

The ebb and flow, the balance of good and evil, exists as part of life. Sometimes, evil rises to feed its black and hungry heart with misery and hate. It is then that the power of good must overcome the beast in whatever shape or form it appears, and return the balance in favour of peace and harmony. Now and again, an evil so dark and vile shows itself with such strength that everything that has been and will be is threatened with extinction.

Lord Maelstrom is that evil. He waits, brooding in darkness, shaping his plans, and gathering his newfound powers. He hungers for revenge and total domination over all things – living and dead – and he *will* have his way.

The final battleground will be the Dimension of Terrae – our world. This blue and green planet that we call Earth.